HER LAST

CHANCE

(A Rachel Gift Mystery—Book Two)

BLAKE PIERCE

Blake Pierce

Blake Pierce is the USA Today bestselling author of the RILEY PAGE mystery series, which includes seventeen books. Blake Pierce is also the author of the MACKENZIE WHITE mystery series, comprising fourteen books; of the AVERY BLACK mystery series, comprising six books; of the KERI LOCKE mystery series, comprising five books; of the MAKING OF RILEY PAIGE mystery series, comprising six books; of the KATE WISE mystery series, comprising seven books; of the CHLOE FINE psychological suspense mystery, comprising six books; of the JESSE HUNT psychological suspense thriller series, comprising nineteen books; of the AU PAIR psychological suspense thriller series, comprising three books; of the ZOE PRIME mystery series, comprising six books; of the ADELE SHARP mystery series, comprising thirteen books, of the EUROPEAN VOYAGE cozy mystery series, comprising four books; of the new LAURA FROST FBI suspense thriller, comprising six books (and counting); of the new ELLA DARK FBI suspense thriller, comprising nine books (and counting); of the A YEAR IN EUROPE cozy mystery series, comprising nine books, of the AVA GOLD mystery series, comprising six books (and counting); and of the RACHEL GIFT mystery series, comprising six books (and counting).

An avid reader and lifelong fan of the mystery and thriller genres, Blake loves to hear from you, so please feel free to visit www.blakepierceauthor.com to learn more and stay in touch.

ALREADY MISSING (Book #4)
ALREADY DEAD (Book #5)
ALREADY TAKEN (Book #6)

EUROPEAN VOYAGE COZY MYSTERY SERIES
MURDER (AND BAKLAVA) (Book #1)
DEATH (AND APPLE STRUDEL) (Book #2)
CRIME (AND LAGER) (Book #3)
MISFORTUNE (AND GOUDA) (Book #4)
CALAMITY (AND A DANISH) (Book #5)
MAYHEM (AND HERRING) (Book #6)

ADELE SHARP MYSTERY SERIES
LEFT TO DIE (Book #1)
LEFT TO RUN (Book #2)
LEFT TO HIDE (Book #3)
LEFT TO KILL (Book #4)
LEFT TO MURDER (Book #5)
LEFT TO ENVY (Book #6)
LEFT TO LAPSE (Book #7)
LEFT TO VANISH (Book #8)
LEFT TO HUNT (Book #9)
LEFT TO FEAR (Book #10)
LEFT TO PREY (Book #11)
LEFT TO LURE (Book #12)
LEFT TO CRAVE (Book #13)

THE AU PAIR SERIES
ALMOST GONE (Book#1)
ALMOST LOST (Book #2)
ALMOST DEAD (Book #3)

ZOE PRIME MYSTERY SERIES
FACE OF DEATH (Book#1)
FACE OF MURDER (Book #2)
FACE OF FEAR (Book #3)
FACE OF MADNESS (Book #4)
FACE OF FURY (Book #5)
FACE OF DARKNESS (Book #6)

A JESSIE HUNT PSYCHOLOGICAL SUSPENSE SERIES

THE PERFECT WIFE (Book #1)
THE PERFECT BLOCK (Book #2)
THE PERFECT HOUSE (Book #3)
THE PERFECT SMILE (Book #4)
THE PERFECT LIE (Book #5)
THE PERFECT LOOK (Book #6)
THE PERFECT AFFAIR (Book #7)
THE PERFECT ALIBI (Book #8)
THE PERFECT NEIGHBOR (Book #9)
THE PERFECT DISGUISE (Book #10)
THE PERFECT SECRET (Book #11)
THE PERFECT FAÇADE (Book #12)
THE PERFECT IMPRESSION (Book #13)
THE PERFECT DECEIT (Book #14)
THE PERFECT MISTRESS (Book #15)
THE PERFECT IMAGE (Book #16)
THE PERFECT VEIL (Book #17)
THE PERFECT INDISCRETION (Book #18)
THE PERFECT RUMOR (Book #19)

CHLOE FINE PSYCHOLOGICAL SUSPENSE SERIES
NEXT DOOR (Book #1)
A NEIGHBOR'S LIE (Book #2)
CUL DE SAC (Book #3)
SILENT NEIGHBOR (Book #4)
HOMECOMING (Book #5)
TINTED WINDOWS (Book #6)

KATE WISE MYSTERY SERIES
IF SHE KNEW (Book #1)
IF SHE SAW (Book #2)
IF SHE RAN (Book #3)
IF SHE HID (Book #4)
IF SHE FLED (Book #5)
IF SHE FEARED (Book #6)
IF SHE HEARD (Book #7)

THE MAKING OF RILEY PAIGE SERIES
WATCHING (Book #1)
WAITING (Book #2)
LURING (Book #3)

TAKING (Book #4)
STALKING (Book #5)
KILLING (Book #6)

RILEY PAIGE MYSTERY SERIES
ONCE GONE (Book #1)
ONCE TAKEN (Book #2)
ONCE CRAVED (Book #3)
ONCE LURED (Book #4)
ONCE HUNTED (Book #5)
ONCE PINED (Book #6)
ONCE FORSAKEN (Book #7)
ONCE COLD (Book #8)
ONCE STALKED (Book #9)
ONCE LOST (Book #10)
ONCE BURIED (Book #11)
ONCE BOUND (Book #12)
ONCE TRAPPED (Book #13)
ONCE DORMANT (Book #14)
ONCE SHUNNED (Book #15)
ONCE MISSED (Book #16)
ONCE CHOSEN (Book #17)

MACKENZIE WHITE MYSTERY SERIES
BEFORE HE KILLS (Book #1)
BEFORE HE SEES (Book #2)
BEFORE HE COVETS (Book #3)
BEFORE HE TAKES (Book #4)
BEFORE HE NEEDS (Book #5)
BEFORE HE FEELS (Book #6)
BEFORE HE SINS (Book #7)
BEFORE HE HUNTS (Book #8)
BEFORE HE PREYS (Book #9)
BEFORE HE LONGS (Book #10)
BEFORE HE LAPSES (Book #11)
BEFORE HE ENVIES (Book #12)
BEFORE HE STALKS (Book #13)
BEFORE HE HARMS (Book #14)

AVERY BLACK MYSTERY SERIES
CAUSE TO KILL (Book #1)

CHAPTER ONE

The suicide gate had been easier to get over than he'd thought. He supposed they were a bit more difficult to navigate when the bridge reached out over the East River, but the gates here, where the Williamsburg Bridge hovered over Brooklyn, were minimal at best. Having gotten past the gates, he was now free to look down to the street, wondering if the drop would be high enough to end his life. He was pretty sure he'd read somewhere that the portion of the bridge that sat over Brooklyn was about one hundred and ten feet from the ground.

That should be enough, right? He hoped so. The only reason he'd waited so long to kill himself was because he feared he'd be one of those poor saps who would somehow do it wrong. He'd put a bullet in his head only to have it somehow not kill him, forcing him to live the rest of his life in a vegetative state. Or, in this case, he'd jump to the street and break both of his legs or fracture his spine, resulting in a life of paralysis.

He'd opted for the street because he felt venturing out over the East River increased his chances of surviving. Really, how hard could water be from just one hundred and thirty feet up? It seemed risky to him— and he figured the hard pavement below was a sure thing.

It was two in the morning, so the darkness made the drop below him seem even farther. He'd chosen this time of the day so no nosy assholes would see him and call the police, but now there was a small part of him that regretted it. If this was indeed his final moment on the planet, it would be nice for *someone* to see it. And right now, the only people he could see was the couple pressed against one of the buildings down below, furiously making out and lost in their own private little world.

He was going to die alone. He'd made the decision to do this but now hated the fact that he'd be doing it with no witnesses.

And why is that?

It was a good question. Jesus, maybe he was being rash. Maybe he wasn't really ready to do this. Surely there was help somewhere out there. He could reach out to his mom and his wife, try to patch things up. He could find some other way out of this. Maybe—

1

Sometimes giving up can be heroic. Sometimes it takes more courage to give up than to lower your head and forge on with something you know just isn't going to work.

That voice was much more pronounced in his head than his own. It was a voice he'd heard on the phone about two hours ago, a comforting and warm voice. *It's your life, so it's also your death,* that voice had also said. *So shouldn't you be in charge of both?*

He looked down to the street, dark and waiting. He could be down there in ten seconds, dead, life over, all of his problems gone.

It was easy to see in his head. He'd probably land face down. His skull would smash, his chest would be shattered, but he'd probably feel very little of it. Still, the imagined sight of it was brutal. God, what the hell was he doing?

"No. No…not now," he told himself. He took a deep breath and turned back to the suicide gate, wondering if he'd be able to scale it. If not, he had his cell phone so he supposed he could call the cops. And wouldn't that be ironic? He'd wanted to avoid having people call the cops to thwart his plans and now here he was, wanting—

The figure on the other side of the gate seemed to come out of nowhere, as if the night itself had manifested it.

"Who—"

But that was all he got out. The figure stepped forward quickly and an arm came through the tight bars of the gate. A hand touched his chest, a gentle push at most, and he felt himself being pitched backwards.

By the time he realized what had happened, he had no time to scream. He drew in the breath but it never came out. In the end, he had been only half right. He indeed died very quickly and the pain was a brief flicker at most; but he died with his face looking up to the Williamsburg Bridge as a halo of blood leaked out from his shattered skull onto the pavement.

CHAPTER TWO

There was something about South Carolina that felt a little *too* southern to Rachel. She knew it was ridiculous, but it was a thought she could not escape. There was the intense pride in southern heritage for one thing, but she was pretty sure it just came down to the humidity. Yes, the summers in Virginia could be brutal, but the humidity a little further south seemed much more oppressive. The damned mosquitos being the size of hummingbirds didn't help either.

She slapped at one as it landed on her Grandma Tate's patio chair. She didn't want to kill it, just scare it away. It went flittering off in search of someone else's blood. As she watched it go flying out over Grandma Tate's acre and a half of back yard, the back door that connected the patio to the kitchen opened up.

Florence Tate came out carrying a pitcher of sweet tea and two large glasses. She was seventy-three, looked closer to sixty, and carried herself like a forty-year-old. Today, she was wearing a sun hat that Rachel *knew* looked ridiculous, but Grandma Tate somehow made it look fashionable. She poured them each a glass of tea, wedges of lemon and rapidly melting ice swirling around inside the pitcher as she poured.

"We can do dinner later," Florence said. "I figure I may as well get the whole danged mess over with. No sense in putting it off now, is it?"

Grandma Tate never had been one for beating around the bush, or, as she had always called it, *pussyfooting.* Yet, for a while there, Rachel had nearly forgotten the whole reason for coming down. Grandma Tate had called last week with a cryptic message, letting her know there was something she needed to say but not over the phone. And when you had elderly loved ones, such a message was never truly a positive thing.

"Well, I've only been here for fifteen minutes," Rachel said. "And in that time, I was guided out to the patio and am now being comforted with what I can assume is some exceptionally sweet tea. That, plus you referring to it as 'a mess' is sort of freaking me out."

Florence waved this away as she sat down in the patio chair next to Rachel. "There you go, going all FBI on me." She chuckled and let out a sigh. When she looked at Rachel, there was a hint of sadness in her eyes, slightly blunted by the shadow of the sun hat falling over her

3

brow. "Over the course of the past three months or so, I've been going back and forth to the doctor," she went on. "As of two weeks ago, I officially have breast cancer."

The suddenness of the way she said it struck Rachel in an odd way. She'd known something bad was coming and she'd also known that Grandma Tate would be blunt about it. But this was a whole new level. It was so disarming that Rachel almost missed the heaviness and seriousness of the news.

"The doctors are sure?" Rachel asked. She was aware that she was already feeling the sting of tears, and a lump was forming in the back of her throat. She'd been close to Grandma Tate in her teenage years but they'd grown apart as Rachel got older. She hadn't seen her grandmother face-to-face in over eight months. But despite that distance, the hurt surprise of the moment was no less real.

"Yes. That's what's been going on for these last few months. Tests to be sure and then to figure out how much time I have and if it's treatable."

"Well, is it?"

"They think it might be. We caught it late, but not the-sky-is-falling late. There's chemo, of course, and some other medicines I don't quite understand. And to be honest with you, I'm not sure if I'm going to look into any of it. The doc basically told me there's nothing much to be done about it."

And then Rachel was crying. Not only that, but the tears seemed to also push another reality to the forefront of her mind. *See how easy that was for her?* some alien voice told her. *She tore that Band-Aid right off and now a loved one knows what she's going through. You could take an example from this…*

Rachel shut the thought out quickly. This was not about her or her diagnosis—this was not about the inoperable tumor that was currently taking up residence inside of her brain. This was about Grandma Tate. And even if she *did* want to tell her grandmother about her own diagnosis, now was not the time. She did not drive all the way down to Aiken, South Carolina, to one-up her with cancer diagnoses.

She sipped from her tea, if only to distract herself. And good Lord, it was about as sweet as she'd imagined it would be—another of those southern things. She eyed her grandmother for a moment and saw that while it had *seemed* easy for her to get the information out, it looked like it had taken an emotion toll. Grandma Tate had a look on her face that was similar to a driver who was coming up on a car accident in the other lane and was trying to decide if they would keep their eyes straight ahead or if they wanted to catch a peek at the damage.

"How long do they give you?" Rachel asked.

"Two years. Maybe three. They say the treatment could cure me, but the chances are slim. And with that treatment, I might get another two years. *Might.* So I figure I'm going to leave these last few years without chemo muddying it all up. And when the end comes…"

She shrugged and sipped from her tea. A mosquito darted around her head and when she swatted at it, her aim was true. It went to the porch floor where she stomped it with her Croc.

Rachel shook her head in disbelief. She reached out and took her grandmother's hand as she had done so many times as a child, as a teenager, and even as they danced slightly inebriated at her wedding reception.

"It's okay, Rachel. Really. I'm at peace with it."

Rachel's own conflicting feelings waged war in her mind. She knew she would not tell her, but the bravery her Grandma Tate was showing made her wonder if she should tell her family. Should she tell Peter and Paige when she returned home, or would it be too much all at once?

"I appreciate you not telling me on the phone," Rachel said. "But at the same time, I just drove seven and a half hours and now this…this is going to hover over the entire visit."

"Well, you're staying until tomorrow, right?"

"Yes."

"Then nothing changes. I say we finish our tea, head out for dinner, and go bowl a few frames."

Rachel couldn't help but laugh. "You're still bowling?"

"Hell yes. My team was second in the spring tournament. Remind me to show you the trophy when we head back inside."

And just like that, the bomb had been dropped. They remained on Florence Tate's patio, drinking tea and swatting at mosquitoes while Rachel shared stories of Paige's adventures and triumphs from school, and how she was growing up *far* too fast. They spoke in the heat and finished the pitcher of tea in about half an hour. The entire time, Rachel felt her own news storming around in her head, stomping at the ground of her thoughts like a rodeo bull anxious to be released from its gate.

She knew then, swatting at mosquitos and trying to wrap her mind around bowling with her cancer-stricken grandmother, that she needed to eventually let it out or it was going to tear her apart inside.

Rachel woke up the following morning with the sound of pins clanging musically together and stared at the ceiling for several minutes before getting out of bed. At some point during the night, she dreamed that Paige, her daughter, had been at the bowling alley with her and Grandma Tate that night. And every time Paige asked a question about Grandma Tate's diagnosis, Rachel would throw a ball down the lane and bowl a very loud strike. The questions went unheard and when it was clear she'd get no answers from the adults, Paige walked away in disappointment.

Rachel's phone was on the nightstand and when she checked it, she saw that it was 5:15. Figuring there was no way she was going to get back to sleep, she quietly made her way into the kitchen.

Grandma Tate was already there. The kitchen smelled of fresh-brewed coffee. She was sitting at the kitchen table, reading from her Bible. Rachel had known that her grandmother believed in God but had never known her to be the type to wake up early to read scripture. Rachel almost decided to back away and leave her grandmother to her quiet time, but she'd already been heard.

Grandma Tate looked her way and smiled. "You don't have to snoop around," she said. Closing the Bible and sliding it to the side, she added, "Grab a cup of coffee and come join me."

Rachel did as asked, mixing her coffee the way she liked and taking the seat opposite her grandmother at the table.

"You always wake up this early?" Rachel asked.

"Every now and then. You?"

"Only when work requires it." Rachel then nodded to the Bible with an uncertain smile on her face. "Is this something you always do or is it because of the diagnosis?"

"No, I don't typically pull it out but it has seemed pertinent these last few months, I guess. I don't even know that it's providing any comfort. It's just something to do, you know? A routine."

Rachel was certain she was lying but said nothing about it. "How can I help?" Rachel asked.

"Just by respecting my wishes. I know it'll get bad at some point. But I don't want the chemo. I don't want to go through that. I need you to accept that and be okay with it."

It stung because she wondered if she'd ever have a similar conversation with her family. Of course, in her case, chemo likely wouldn't even work. Her doctor had pretty much come out and said it.

The tumor in her head seemed to thrum in response to this thought. She knew it really wasn't thrumming or moving or speaking, but she sensed it in that moment, all the same.

"I can do that," she said as the guilt continued to pierce her.

"And we can also set up a time for me to come visit to see that great-granddaughter of mine."

"Yes, I can help with that, too."

Florence sipped from her coffee and got to her feet. "And now, because you're an early bird like me, I say we get in the kitchen and make breakfast. How about French toast?"

"I don't know if I can eat French toast after that second dinner we had at the lanes last night."

"I bet you can," Grandma Tate said, already heading for the kitchen. "Besides, I want you to have a full stomach when you pull out of here in a few hours."

Together, they got out all of the ingredients and, just like the night before, there was no talk of Florence's diagnosis. As Rachel cracked eggs into a bowl, she watched her grandmother mixing up brown sugar and cinnamon, a genuine smile on her face.

Two years, Rachel thought. *That's longer than I've got. I hope she enjoys every day of it.*

With that thought, the only thing that kept the tears from spilling was the smile on Grandma Tate's face despite the grim future that awaited her. But even that bit of joy was overshadowed by her own wretched secret, a truth that seemed to already be peeling apart her thoughts and dreams of the future while looking for a way out into the light.

If anything, though, it made her more anxious to get back home to see Peter and Paige. Yes, she was still wrestling with her secret diagnosis, but she also knew that she could take a lesson from Grandma Tate. Maybe telling them would be okay. Maybe she could be brave and strong like Grandma Tate.

Maybe it was time to tell them after all.

CHAPTER THREE

She only made a single stop during the seven-and-a-half-hour drive, and that was for a quick snack and to fill up with gas. Perhaps it was the bowling dream or just the overwhelming wait of her own diagnosis now coupled with Grandma Tate's, but she very badly wanted to see Paige. She wanted to see Peter, too, of course, but her heart ached to see her daughter.

Because she'd woken up so early and left almost two full hours before she'd originally planned, she arrived home just shy of four o'clock. The house was empty, as it was Thursday and Peter would have taken Paige to soccer practice. It was the one time of the week he intentionally took time off of work to spend daddy-daughter time with her. The routine was soccer, a quick stop for ice cream, and then home to help mommy with dinner.

Standing in the empty living room for two whole minutes, Rachel almost left the house and headed over to the soccer fields but knew that was silly. They'd be home in less than half an hour. She sat at the kitchen counter contemplating an early glass of wine when she thought of the ease in which Grandma Tate had made her decision to not pursue any treatments. It was a decision Rachel had made in her own mind but had yet to confirm with her doctor. If she truly did only have a year or so left, she'd be damned if she'd spend that bit of time hooked to machines and in a constant state of pain and nausea. More than that, she did not want her daughter's last vision of her to be a ruin of the woman she'd once been.

While she had the nerve to do so, she pulled her phone from her pocket and called her doctor's office, using the number from the business card that had come in the initial packet of information following her diagnosis. It was answered on the second ring by a soft, pleasant voice.

"Dr. Greene's office, how can we help today?"

"Is Dr. Greene available by any chance?"

"No, I'm sorry," the receptionist said. Her polite tone made Rachel feel she truly was sorry. "He's with a patient right now and he has another immediately after that. Could I take a message?"

Rachel almost said no, but then figured this might be something of an out for her. "Sure. It's pretty important that he gets it and that it's accurate, though. Is that okay?"

"Of course. I'll type it up right now. What's the message?"

"My name is Rachel Gift, and I've decided to not undergo any treatments based on my current diagnosis."

There was the briefest hesitation on the other line and when the receptionist did speak, she lacked some of the warmth that had been in her voice only moments ago. "Yes, okay, I've got that. Would you like Dr. Greene to call you back?"

"He can if he'd like to, but it's not necessary. Thank you."

"Okay, then," the receptionist said, still not quite herself. "You have a great afternoon."

Rachel hung up, surprised to find just how much freedom she now felt as a result of the call. It was as if vocalizing it—even if just to her doctor's receptionist—made it more real. It helped her to understand how Grandma Tate had been able to break the news so easily.

With her phone still in her hand, Rachel opened up her Notes app. She thought of bowling with Grandma Tate and eating that delicious, greasy food. All small things, but enjoyable. It was how Grandma Tate seemed to want to spend the rest of her days. With that in mind, Rachel starting typing, making a list.

The first item was **Paris**. Then, without even thinking too hard about it, the next item on her list was **reconcile with dad**. She looked at that one for several moments, wondering where the hell it had even come from. She'd given up any hope of mending that relationship years ago. And the bastard likely wouldn't even meet with her or be interested in any sort of reconciliation anyway. It had been over ten years since she'd seen him and as far as she was concerned, it would be the last.

To get away from those thoughts, she continued the list with a third item: **Disney trip for Paige**. She was thinking of what other items to include in this written record of what she wanted to get done before she died when she heard the front door opening. She closed the app and pocketed her phone as she walked into the living room to meet her family. When she saw Paige enter through the doorway, she got choked up and did her best not to rush the girl and sweep her up in a dramatic embrace.

Instead, she knelt down and opened her arms as naturally as possible. Paige came rushing to her in her soccer outfit while Peter came in behind her. She wondered if they'd ever looked more perfect.

9

Paige was the spitting image of her father, their dark hair and slightly pointed chins hard to miss. As Paige came in with her bright smile and her short-cut hair bobbing up and down, Peter trailed behind, carrying his briefcase as well as Paige's school bookbag. As he watched his daughter and wife hugging, he said, "You're home earlier than I expected."

"I left earlier than I'd planned," she said. She released Paige and then hugged Peter. As she kissed him softly on the cheek, he whispered in her ear. He asked a question and even though it was not *about* her, she felt guilty. And she knew exactly why.

"How is she? Is everything okay?"

"Come in the kitchen with me, would you?" she asked. They broke the hug and Rachel instantly looked to Paige. "You got homework?"

"Just a little bit. One worksheet."

"Okay. Listen…I need to talk to Daddy about private grown-up stuff for just a few minutes. Can you go ahead and knock that worksheet out while we talk in the kitchen?"

The frown on her face indicated that she was not a fan of this idea, but Paige nodded. She took the bookbag from her father and unzipped it, rummaging around for the worksheet. Rachel took Peter by the hand and led him into the kitchen. She could see by the grim expression on his face that he pretty much already knew bad news was coming.

Rachel leaned against the kitchen counter and Peter stood close to her. "Are you okay?" he whispered.

"I am, yes. But Grandma Tate found out that she has breast cancer. They caught it on the late side and she's made the decision to not get any treatments for it."

Peter looked baffled for a moment but did a good job of keeping his voice low when he said, "No treatments? Why did she make that decision?"

"She doesn't want her final days muddied and messy by medicines that *might* only give her another year or so." She smiled thinly and added: "She truly seems at peace with it."

"So how long does she have?"

"A year and a half. Maybe two years at most."

"Oh my God," Peter said. He looked back into the living room, making sure Paige had not decided to play spy. "Does she need anything?"

"Not right now, no. Just our support and to help plan a weekend or so when she can come up and see Paige for a while."

"Do you think we tell Paige? Or should we leave that for your grandmother?"

"I think we leave it to Grandma Tate. And we could be there to help answer questions about what it all means."

They both looked out to the living room then, where Paige was obediently filling out her worksheet at the coffee table. "Well, when it gets to the…to the *end*, we'll do whatever we can," Peter said. "Anything we can do to make her comfortable, you know?"

Rachel nodded, wondering what his reaction would be if she came forward with her own diagnosis. The stress, the worry…it would be terrible. And then there would be trying to explain it to Paige. The idea of it broke her heart and she had to look away from her.

"You're okay, for real?" Peter asked.

"Yeah. Like I said, she seemed to be in a really good place with it."

"Well, if it's too heavy and the drive back was too much, we can cancel our plans tonight. What do you think?"

"Plans?" But as soon as she said it, she remembered. "Shit, that's right. Terry's birthday party. I totally forgot."

"I'll call him and tell him we can't make it."

"No, let's go. And maybe you can drive. I think a few drinks with friends might be exactly what I need right now. Do you think you can call the sitter?"

"Yes, I can drive. And I'll call the sitter."

"And maybe order pizza for dinner?" Rachel said. "I think I'd like to spend the evening with Paige before we go. I missed her quite a bit while I was in Aiken."

"It was just two days. You're gone longer on bureau trips…a lot longer sometimes." There was concern in his voice, and a bit of warmth. Peter always liked it when Rachel was verbal about how much she missed them when she was away for a case. She wasn't the most vulnerable of people, and he latched on to this show of emotion whenever it raised its head.

"I know," she said, struggling with tears. "Maybe it was just the news, or Grandma Tate focusing on trying to spend some time with her."

Peter leaned forward and kissed her softly on the mouth. "Do what you need to do. I'll call the pizza in."

Rachel walked slowly back into the living room, giving herself time to regroup. She sat on the couch by Paige and saw that the worksheet was for counting by fives. Paige was nearly done, her little tongue sticking out in concentration.

I won't be here much longer, kiddo, she thought as she watched her work. *You deserve to have a mother, but you don't deserve the pain of learning that you're going to lose her far too early. I don't know what to do and I'm so afraid you're going to suffer because of my cowardice.*

She kept it all inside, though, sitting on it as if she were hiding a bomb that might very well explode at any moment. She knew it would blow at any given moment, but her concern was keeping her family safe when it did.

CHAPTER FOUR

"Peter! Rachel!"

Terry McCreedy greeted them as they came in through his front door. "Drinks are in the kitchen, food is on the counter, and the last thirty-five years of my life are…" He stopped here, looked dramatically behind him, and then shrugged. "Well, I don't know where the fuck they went!"

Terry did not look thirty-five. He looked closer to twenty-five, the type of guy who looked like he might be on his way out the door to go surfing in Maui or cliff diving in South America. Tonight, his long blond hair was pulled back in a ponytail, as if to ward off the northern end of the thirties, keeping forty as far away as possible.

Terry had been Peter's college roommate during their freshman and sophomore years. They'd stayed in touch after graduation, both remaining around the Richmond area, and tended to hang out at least once a month, either catching a movie or getting together on a hiking trail. Rachel liked Terry quite a bit because he was goofy beyond measure and she was pretty sure it was where the small and barely-still-remaining childish side of Peter came from.

As they stepped inside the apartment, Rachel found that it was exactly the sort of thing she'd needed. She could already hear boisterous laughter, the soft thumping of '90s hip-hop, and the clinking of glass bottles. Rachel and Peter made their way through the party, which looked to be small but energetic. There were four couples (three married and one just dating) and a few singles (including Terry himself) scattered around. The Gifts made the rounds with drinks in hand and were instantly stopped by the Youngs. Married for three years now, they were the sort of couple who thought they had marriage figured out because the first few years still felt magical.

"Holy crap," Mark Young said. "Rachel Gift makes an appearance!"

"I know," Peter said. "I polished her up really nice and figured I'd bring her out for a ride around the block."

"Ooh, you may be making that ride back home alone with talk like that," Rachel said.

"How's the job?" Mark asked.

"Great. Killing bad guys every day, and tapping *so many* phones. You know how it goes."

She did her best to keep conversation feeling lively and fresh but the truth of the matter was that Rachel always felt as if she were some sort of outcast in situations like these. She was the one who had a job everyone seemed to be enamored with but didn't want to ask too many questions about. Even tonight, as they made their rounds, the questions remained limited to how much travel she'd done and generic one-liners about catching bad guys or if she knew any Jack Bauer types. She took it all in stride and did her best to be as social and as friendly as possible. It was harder than she thought it would be, as her mind kept trying to remind her that she was really only here to try to bury her own recent bad news as well as Grandma Tate's.

The social interactions went a long way to help with that. All of the conversations she and Peter had were surface-level, as they had never really taken the time to connect or go deep with another couple. They had lots of friends, but no *good* friends. And that was fine with both of them, as it was one of the many things they had in common. Even back in their dating days, neither had been too concerned with making lifelong friends.

Knowing full well that Mark and Peter were going to delve into conversations about Peter's job as a proposal expert for a telecommunications firm, Rachel delicately sidestepped away. "I think I'm going to go grab us some drinks," she said.

Peter gave her hand a squeeze as she left his side. She noticed that he gave a careful look as she left, as if making sure she was really okay with being here. She smiled at him but the harsh truth was that she was already regretting the decision to come out. She would have much rather not called a sitter and stayed home with Paige. Of course, it was too late to act on that now. She figured they'd stay another half an hour, make a point to talk to Terry at least one more time, and slip out. Yes, it would be early but all she'd have to do was make an excuse about work. No one would ask and no one would pry.

She found the coolers in the kitchen and rummaged around in one. She grabbed an Amstel for her and a Bud Light for Peter, and started on her way out. As she did, though, she noticed the three people sitting at the table. One was a man, speaking in an almost cheerful way about what he was referring to as "utter bullshit." The woman beside him was laughing uneasily.

Sitting across the table from both of them was a woman with sleek red hair. She looked to be in her late twenties or so and was taking the man's accusations of "utter bullshit" with a grain of salt. It wasn't until Rachel took a step closer to the table on her way out that she noticed the red-haired woman had a set of tarot cards spread out on the table in front of her. The woman looked to be in the middle of a reading—*his* reading—and the man was ridiculing her the whole way. He shook his head, chuckling, and got up from the table. He wasn't being rude, just letting the tarot reader know this clearly was not for him. The girl beside him also got up, giving the reader an apologetic smile as she chased off after the man.

This left Rachel alone in the kitchen with the tarot reader. As she started gathering her cards back up and shuffling them into a single pile, she looked at Rachel and smiled. "You want a reading?"

"Oh, no thank you."

Right away, she heard Peter approach her from behind. He put a hand on her waist and whispered in her ear. "I think it could be fun."

She turned to him and said, "Then you get one."

"Oh, I will. You first, though. Come on. It's just some silly fun."

Rachel considered it for a moment. Had she not witnessed the first couple get up and leave in such a dismissive way, she would have probably ignored Peter's persuasions. But she almost felt sorry for the reader—even though Rachel herself did not believe in tarot, crystals, or any of that other New Age stuff. She took Peter's hand and led him to the table. As he pulled out a chair for herself, she looked to the reader. "Sure. Let's do a reading."

"Fantastic," the tarot reader said. "I'm Margo, by the way."

"Rachel," she said, giving a polite little nod.

Margo nodded right back and instantly started shuffling the cards. She did so with the skill one might expect to see from a dealer at a Vegas casino. She barely even looked at the cards, but took in the room. She seemed to study Peter quite hard, as if making sure he wasn't going to start mocking the process. After about twenty seconds or so of very precise shuffling, Margo took a deep breath, held it for a moment, and then closed her eyes as she flipped the top card off of the deck, but not over on its back just yet.

"Is there a question you have about your current journey?" Margo asked. "We must ask the deck a question before it can provide an answer."

Rachel was already starting to feel a bit cheesy, so she went with the first question that came to mind. "I have a sick grandmother," she said, making sure not to reveal the ailment. "I'd like to know if her last year or so of life will be a happy one."

15

With her eyes still closed, Margo took yet another deep breath and this time flipped the card over. She then laid four more cards on the table, facedown. She opened her eyes and looked at the first card she'd set down, already turned up and facing them. Rachel also looked at it and saw a simple illustration of the moon.

"The Moon card," Margo said. "Quite simple, but it could mean any number of things."

She then ran her fingers slowly across the other four cards she'd laid facedown. Her fingers slowed, and she paused on the one all the way to the left. She flipped it over, tilted her head, and made a *hmmm* sound.

"This is the High Priestess. For women, it is often a good card to have but if you are talking about sickness it can be the very opposite. Do you know if there is some sort of hidden sickness your grandmother is not yet telling you about?"

"Not that I'm aware of. She just told me about *this* sickness yesterday."

"I see," Margo said, studying the High Priestess card a bit longer before turning over the one beside it. When she did, her eyes went wide for a moment. Rachel could not deny that she, too, did not like what she saw. "This is the Devil," Margo said. "I know it can seem scary, but it is not always a portent of evil. It can often simply refer to struggles or secrets. With the Moon and the High Priestess…I feel something akin to trickery involved in this sickness. Maybe she is not telling you everything. Let's see…"

Rachel knew it was silly, but a little flicker of dread passed through her. It wasn't fear, but a general sort of uneasiness.

Margo flipped the next card, leaving only one more. The newly flipped card was no better than the previous one. The skeleton holding a scythe on the front told Rachel all she needed to know. And although she did not believe in any of this, it still made her very uneasy.

"Death" Margo said. "This sickness…" She ran her hand back to the High Priestess and hovered there for a moment. "Is it cancer? Is she expecting to die from it?"

The accuracy was spooky, and a chill went up Rachel's spine. She only nodded, not allowing herself to speak. In a strange way, she felt like she'd be almost gossiping about her grandmother's illness if she spoke it out loud to this woman she did not know.

Margo now had a grim look on her face. It almost seemed as if she wanted to stop. She took a bit longer to reach for the last card. When she flipped it, she seemed very confused at first and then she looked to

Rachel with a bit of bite in her stare. If the woman was putting on an act just for effect, she was doing a damn good job.

"This is the Fool," Margo said. She still looked genuinely confused, looking back and forth between the cards and then to Rachel again. "With the Moon and the Devil, this does indeed point to trickery of some kind. Throw in Death and…it redirects the entire thing to the person who asked a question of the deck."

Rachel found herself unable to speak, but Peter asked the very thing she was thinking. She was relieved to hear the skepticism in his voice. "Meaning what, exactly?"

"That death is in your future, Rachel." She stopped here, her bottom lip quivering a bit. She looked confused, maybe even a little scared. Whether or not this was all an act, it was clear that Margo was not saying this lightly. "And based on what I see here, it may be very soon."

"Well," Peter said, clapping his hands one single time. "That's certainly very cheerful but it's also a fine example of how I'm not right all the time. No way in hell should we have done this reading. Her grandmother *is* sick. So thanks for this little burst of sunshine."

"Wait," Margo said, her voice a little shaky now. "One more card to round it out."

"I think you've done enough," Peter said. He was getting irritated, which was not something Rachel had expected. He took Rachel by the hand, clearly upset. As Rachel got to her feet, she could not take her eyes away from the cards. She watched as Margo flipped a fourth card. And though Rachel, now being led out of the kitchen, could not see the card, Margo explained its meaning.

"There is also unforgiveness in your future. Perhaps because of this sickness."

Rachel remained quiet, but Peter, angry beyond belief now, had a quick retort. "Go to hell."

Peter led her out of the kitchen, where the rest of the party was in full swing. Rachel looked one last time back at Margo and did her best to ignore the look of abject fear on the woman's face.

"You okay?" Peter asked as they joined the rest of the party.

"Yeah. That was just spooky as hell. That's all."

"I know. Sorry. I shouldn't have even suggested it. With Grandma Tate and everything, I should have known better."

"It's okay," she said.

"I mean, you don't buy into that bullshit anyway, right?"

"No," she said, doing her best to show him a smile. "Not at all. But I do want to get out of here. Can we start saying goodbyes?"

"Of course."

That's exactly what they did. Yet even as they said goodbye to their friends and wished Terry one final Happy Birthday, Rachel could not shake the chill she'd encountered while sitting across from Margo as she flipped over the cards. And even beyond that, she felt like she'd dodged a bullet; if Peter even remotely believed in tarot readings and other mysticisms, they may be having a very hard talk right now.

Even the idea of that thought leveled her inside, killing any hope that she'd be able to show some of Grandma Tate's tenacity and coming clean with her family.

***

Paige was deeply asleep when they arrived home, with her favorite teddy bear tucked under her arm and her noise-maker playing Whispering Stream, her favorite. While Peter paid the sitter and shut off the lights, Rachel lay down next to Paige, spooning her. She felt the rise and fall of her breathing, closing her eyes and just breathing the moment in. It was so calming that Rachel nearly fell asleep right there (the sounds of Whispering Stream certainly did nothing to help). It was only the sound of Peter coming up the stairs that made her get up.

They met in the bedroom, where Peter took her in his arms. "Sorry about the tarot nonsense…again."

"It's okay. Really."

"And sorry about Grandma Tate, too. Maybe we can sit down tomorrow and figure out a good time for her to visit."

"That would be good."

She hoped this would be the last thing he'd say. She was too distracted by the tarot cards, how Margo had looked genuinely afraid. And then the near revelation, how Margo, who did not know her at all, had somehow known that *she* was sick. Sure it could have been a coincidence, a tarot reader just trying to get a chill from a party guest…but it hadn't *felt* like it.

Oh, and let's not forget your imprisoned friend Alex Lynch figured it out, too. And he was able to tell just by seeing you and paying attention to your mannerisms.

Images of infamous serial killer Alex Lynch were the last things she wanted in her head while she lay in bed next to her husband. She was able to dash those images, but they were only replaced by recollections of her visit to see Grandma Tate and then the stupid tarot cards. At some point during the swarm of thoughts, Rachel turned to the bedside clock and saw that it had somehow come to be 2:50 in the morning. She'd had many sleepless nights since getting her diagnosis, and it seemed this was going to be another one.

She gave up just shy of 3:30 and snuck downstairs. There, she boiled some water and had a cup of lemon ginger tea—something she'd learned helped to gradually stir her fully awake in the face of a day that was going to be long and tiring. She'd brought her phone down, intending to scroll through Facebook and read the news. Instead, she ended up opening the bucket list she'd started earlier in the day.

The tears came before she knew it and Rachel had to put the phone down. For that reason, it scared the hell out of her when it rang. With a little yelp, and swallowing back a tide of sorrow, she picked it up. She saw the time—4:12—and was therefore not at all surprised to see that it was Director Anderson. He was calling from his mobile number, not the desk in his office, so she assumed he'd been rudely awakened by a call for assistance on a case. And for some reason, it appeared that she and Jack were the agents he always chose to throw at those early morning cases. Probably because they were still considered relatively young.

She answered quickly, hoping the initial ring of the phone had not stirred Paige awake. She walked quickly to the laundry room just off the kitchen as she answered, closing the door to hide her voice from the rest of the house.

"This is Agent Gift," she said.

"Sorry for the late call, Gift. I got a call about a case that I think you and Rivers would be a good fit on. It's in New York, so I need you to get a move on as soon as possible. Looks to be an ugly one and if there *is* a serial on our hands here, he's moving fast. I've got HR booking the flights right now."

"New York?" she asked, a bit surprised. It was rare that Anderson ever sent agents from Richmond out any farther than Baltimore, Maryland, or Raleigh, North Carolina.

"Yeah, I know it's a hike. But it looks to be a series of jumpers that may not have actually jumped. Three in as many days, and this latest one seems more like a murder than a jump."

This made more sense. She and Jack had worked two cases like this in the past year and a half—supposed suicides that ended up being staged murders. One had been with the use of shotguns to the head while the others had been hangings. She really hoped this wasn't going to be the sort of thing that she and Jack became known for.

"I'm having the police, autopsy, and forensics reports sent to you and Rivers. Check in when you get to the Big Apple, would you?"

"Yes, sir."

She ended the call and took a moment for herself, standing in the laundry room and letting it all soak in. There was her own diagnosis, then there was Grandma Tate's terrible news, the peculiar moment with the tarot reader, and her sudden urge to grieve over the time she was not going to have to spend with her daughter.

If you're going to be dead in a year and a half, you need to quit this job, she told herself. *You need to quit, tell Peter and Paige what's going on, and spend your last days with them. At least Grandma Tate is going out her own way, stress free and relaxed.*

But Rachel would not allow herself to dwell on any of it for too long. Right now, she needed to distract herself. And this case in New York would be perfect for that.

Sure, keep distracting yourself. This time, the voice belonged to Grandma Tate, and even in Rachel's head the old woman was snarky. *Keep distracting yourself and you'll end up distracting yourself right into your grave.*

With a heavy sigh, Rachel left the laundry room and looked to the stairs. She made sure she wasn't going to break down in tears anytime soon before climbing them to tell Peter about her sudden trip to New York, and to get in one more quick snuggle with Paige.

After all, there was no guarantee just how many more she was going to get.

CHAPTER FIVE

Their flight was schedule to leave Richmond International Airport at 6:22, which gave Rachel and Jack very little time to catch up or even grab a bite to eat in the airport on the way to their gate. Jack was his usual vibrant self, in a good mood and seemingly excited about a trip to New York. Even this early in the morning, he had that same boyish charm to him. His brown hair had been lazily combed and was still somewhat of a mess but it somehow fit him well.

Rachel did her best to hide how tired she truly was as she continued to check her phone to see if Anderson had emailed them the reports yet. She saw that they'd just come in when they arrived at their gate. The first group of passengers had already been called.

"The bureau sure knows how to cut this stuff close, don't they?" Jack asked. "You look tired, Rachel. Not enough sleep?"

"Not by a long shot. I came back from a trip to South Carolina to see my grandmother and then went to a birthday party. And now there's this." She left out the part about freaking out about her diagnosis, as well as that of Grandma Tate's, of course.

"Let's tear through these reports on the plane quickly, then," Jack said. "Maybe afterwards, you can grab a nap."

"I'll be okay," she said as they meandered out onto the airbridge. "I'm just really hoping this whole suicide-that-looks-like-a-murder thing doesn't become our normal gig."

Jack chuckled, but Rachel knew he likely wouldn't mind this. He'd been looking for some sort of specialty to sink his teeth into ever since they'd first worked together. He very much wanted to be the expert in a certain field who would be called out for cases all around the country. And it didn't seem like he was too picky about what that field might be.

They didn't bother looking through the reports until they were in the air and leveled out, not wanting to be interrupted by all of the announcements. When they finally pulled it all up on their phones, it was pretty much exactly what Anderson had told her.

Three people, all men, had died from apparent suicides by jumping off of bridges in the past three days. Based on everything Rachel read in the reports, the first two had very strong evidence to support straightforward suicides. But the third, which had occurred just the night before on the Williamsburg Bridge, wasn't quite as cut and dry. First of all, the trajectory and point of impact for the body was totally off. Second, there was an eyewitness who saw the fall and claimed there looked like a second person up on the bridge moments after the man had fallen.

"So here's my first question," Jack said. "I wonder how often people go out to those bridges to kill themselves. I know many go out to do it and then chicken out. But in a city the size of New York, is a bridge jumper really all that uncommon?"

"It's a good question, for sure," Rachel said. "I think I even read a statistic somewhere along the way that something like three people a week at least attempt to throw themselves off of the George Washington Bridge."

"That seems a bit high."

"Well, there are a lot of people in New York City. Of course, that leads to another interesting thing. The George Washington Bridge wasn't the site for any of these. These are mostly smaller, lesser-known bridges. If you look at this second one, it took place just barely outside of the city, right between New York City and Cold Spring. The jumper jumped from a much smaller bridge and struck the rocks below. So could you even pinpoint that one to the city?"

"I would," Jack said. "I'd say it's close enough. The incidents are all rather spread out, too…not just fixated on one single bridge."

"Well, one thing is for sure: the autopsy reports all seem to agree that they were all suicides. Angles of the fall, the lack of any evidence of an altercation of any kind on the scene. It makes me wonder why local PD would think it's urgent enough to warrant an FBI presence."

"They're probably just playing it safe. If this third guy *does* turn out to be a homicide then everyone is going to start wondering about the others. And if there's a killer out there that's somehow tracking suicidal people, that's going to be a weird case. It would also have the potential to bring up rumors of a serial killer. So bringing us in and conducting a proper investigation into those rumors before they start *would* be a good idea."

Rachel grinned as she sipped from her complimentary airline orange juice. "That's all very well thought out."

"I thought so. And if you don't mind me saying so, it's usually the sort of thing *you'd* think of and mention right away. You seem distracted. Everything okay?"

22

She instantly heard this as an echo of all of his questions from the last case they'd worked on. Jack had instantly sensed that something was off and her reluctance to be honest with him had caused quite a bit of strain between them. She supposed she could be at least partially honest this time and tell him about her visit to Aiken to see Grandma Tate.

"Yeah, I guess I am a little distracted," she said. She debated for a moment if she wanted to tell him everything, so she settled on the basics. "I just found out yesterday that my grandmother has cancer. They caught it with decent time remaining, but she's refusing treatment."

"God, Rachel, I'm so sorry. Were you close to her?"

"Sort of." She left it at that. It would take too much time to really give him a proper summary of Grandma Tate—the woman who had essentially raised her as a girl after her mother died and her father moved away to parts unknown.

It was odd, but she felt some of what she'd experienced when telling Peter. She felt like she was flirting with coming too close to her own truths. It felt like opening a door that was going to cause a lot of trouble if it wasn't closed very soon.

"I'm really sorry to hear that. I guess I'd be pretty distracted, too."

"She seems at peace with it, so I guess that's the important thing."

Rachel left it at that, once again turning her attention to her phone where she started to reread the police reports. She hoped it would be enough to communicate that she didn't really want to talk about it anymore and Jack, always observant, picked up on it. After one more read-through, she even tried Jack's suggestion of stealing a quick nap before they touched down. She dozed only briefly, stirred awake for the final time by the sound of the captain announcing their descent toward JFK.

CHAPTER SIX

The investigating detective on the case was out on patrol when they contacted him so they didn't meet at the station. Instead, they met at a small coffee shop several blocks away from the Williamsburg Bridge. This was perfectly fine with Rachel, as she needed the caffeine boost and had not yet eaten anything substantial for breakfast. The detective's name was Branson, and he had the look of a guy who never quite got enough sleep and overcompensated to make it appear otherwise. He was ruggedly handsome, his late-thirties face outlined in a five o'clock shadow that looked like it might have been spray-painted on. His black hair was closely cropped, making him look a bit younger than he likely was.

After initial introductions, they sat down at a table in the back. "I figure I can take you over to the Williamsburg Bridge first," he said. "It's the only one of the sites that makes it look like there might have been foul play—a third party, or something. And it's just enough to make you wonder if the other two might have been a little off as well."

"Clear something up for us, would you?" Jack said. "Agent Gift says she read somewhere that three people each week attempt to throw themselves off of the George Washington Bridge. How accurate is that?"

"Pretty accurate, I'd say," Branson said. He sipped from his coffee and shrugged. "Around the holidays it's more."

"And when we say 'attempt,' what does that mean, exactly?"

"Most of the time, someone will see an individual trying to get out past the suicide gates or barriers and call it in to the police. The majority of the time, the police talk them out of it. Other times, the would-be jumper will change their minds while they're out there and either call the cops themselves or wave down a passerby and have them call for help."

"The report says that for the third jumper, there was a witness down below that may have seen a second person up there. Were you able to speak with them?"

"Yes, and her account is muddy at best. She said she heard a yelping sound that she assumed was the man falling. When she looked up, she said she saw the falling body first, but then saw what she *thought* was a fleeting shadow up on the edge of the bridge. There one minute and gone the next. She said it looked like it was a figure running off. And that's all we got."

"The yelp seems weird to me," Rachel said. "If he was up there to jump, where would the yelp come from? You'd think he'd only cry out in surprise, right?"

"Right. And it's another reason this one on the Williamsburg Bridge seems fishy to me."

"Are there any details from the first two that stick out to you?" Jack asked.

"A few, but I don't want to get too far ahead of myself. I will say that the case of the man that died falling off of the Ramble Bridge in Cold Spring did not seem to fit the profile of someone wanting to end his life. But we'll cross that bridge when we get there." Branson smirked at the wordplay and Rachel had to admit that it was morbidly funny.

"Anyway, if you guys are ready, we can head out to the Williamsburg Bridge. I'll drive."

They all got up and headed for the door. Rachel took the steps and felt a vague swaying in her head. She winced and stopped walking for a moment, waiting for those familiar white streaks to appear across her vision. But the sensation of vertigo passed quickly and after a few moments, it all went back to normal. Jack, a few steps ahead of her as he followed after Branson, hadn't noticed.

Slightly nervous, Rachel caught up as Branson held the door open for them. Rachel smiled appreciatively, though she could not help but feel that even though they had not yet even properly started the case, she'd already dodged a bullet.

***

As they walked to the place along the side of the bridge where the third man had presumably climbed out over the suicide barriers less than forty-eight hours ago, Rachel looked to the left and saw the expanse of the Williamsburg Bridge. Out that way, it would connect Manhattan's Lower East Side with the area of Brooklyn that sat below them. Rachel wasn't overly familiar with New York City, but she was quite certain the neighborhood itself was called Williamsburg. Somewhere behind them, the Brooklyn-Queens expressway buzzed with life.

"Right here," Branson said, standing behind Rachel and slightly to the right, "was where the eyewitness said she saw the second figure. "The place where the two of you are currently standing is where it's believed the jumper, Edwin Newkirk, jumped from. But as you read in the report, he made some pretty good distance. It's the primary reason we think he was pushed. Unless he was expressly trying to see how far out he could jump, it just doesn't add up."

Rachel looked at the so-called suicide gates in front of her. It was little more than a gate—really just one more layer of deterrent from a would-be jumper. In other words, you'd have to be pretty determined to really get out there to the edge and jump.

"But if there were a second person," Rachel said, "they'd have to be on the other side of the gates." Experimentally, she reached her arm through the steel rails of the gate. She *supposed* someone could reach out and give a shove, but it would take one hell of a stretch.

"I thought the same thing," Branson said. "But people get very creative with this stuff. There have been a few folks that have skipped these gates altogether, forgoing the edge. Some have climbed up the suspension towers." He pointed up over their heads and said, "That's a three-hundred-and-fifty-foot drop from up there."

Jack stared out from beside her, looking through the rails. "You see that?" he asked, pointing to the outer wall of the bridge's edging. "Right there, on that little lip facing us. Those are scuff marks, aren't they?"

She'd noticed them too, but thought they were likely nothing more than wear and tear on the old bridge. But the more she looked at them, the more she agreed; they looked like scuff marks from shoes scrambling for purchase as someone tried to crawl up on that outer edge—the final piece of the bridge before free fall and open air. She counted at least four in all, and another two marks that may or may not have been sneaker scuff marks.

"I can't tell if any of them are fresh," she said.

Rachel then found herself reaching up and feeling along the top of the suicide gate. She looked down to the Brooklyn streets below, imagining a man falling from this height. In doing so, she imagined herself falling, the air rushing past her as she anticipated a violent yet brief smashing sensation as she connected with the pavement.

For a moment, she closed her eyes at the thought and realized there was an odd sort of peace to it. The idea of jumping, the idea of release and falling, then the waiting darkness and…nothing. No more hiding her diagnosis, no more wrestling with the reality of cancer ending her life. She could fall blissfully and experience pain for a split second and be done with it all.

She opened her eyes, terrified at how alluring the idea of it was. Slowly, she released her hands from the gate and took a few steps away. "What do we know about the jumper?" she asked. "Did he live here?"

"In Brooklyn, yes. Not really near the bridge, though. Still…if you're suicidal and living in Brooklyn, I guess this bridge is going to come to mind."

Rachel looked back down to the street, thinking of the sort of determination it would take to climb the gate and get out there.

The fall, the release, the end…

She closed her eyes again, this time trying to usher the idea away. "I think I'd like to talk to his family," she said. "The report said he was married, right?"

"Yes. And the wife honestly didn't seem like it was much of a surprise that he'd do this. He'd been having a rough time lately."

Rachel nodded, finally managing to center her mind back on the case. And it all came back to the eyewitness hearing the yelp of surprise just before she saw the body falling. She'd have to talk to the coroner or someone with Forensics in terms of the trajectory of the falling body and how it made no sense but for now, the report of that cry of surprise was enough for her.

Without saying another word, Rachel started walking slowly back the way they had come. Looking through the rails to the street below, she realized she could almost identify with a willing jumper. And with that realization, she found herself in a desperate hurry to get the hell off the bridge.

CHAPTER SEVEN

When Rachel knocked on the door of the Newkirks' apartment, the wife answered the door quickly. The modest apartment sat just a mile and a half away from the Williamsburg Bridge and Rachel could swear she could still feel the shadow of the bridge on her.

The wife was dressed in a Giants T-shirt and a pair of sweatpants. While it did not look like she'd been crying a lot, her eyes did have a tired sort of glaze to them. She regarded Branson, Rachel, and Jack with a cursory nod as she invited them into her home. She led them into the kitchen, where she'd apparently been in the middle of eating a late breakfast of fruit and oatmeal. She resumed her meal without much thought in front of her three visitors.

"Hannah Newkirk, these are Agents Gift and Rivers, with the FBI," Branson said. "They're out of Richmond, Virginia, and have some experience with cases like Edwin's."

"Suicides?" Hannah asked, spooning at her oatmeal. "Jumpers?"

"Deaths that look like suicides at first glance," Jack explained.

"Detective Branson has told us about the oddities surrounding your husband's case," Rachel said.

"And I know it's been painful to already tell me all you could," Branson said, "but I thought it might be best if you told them yourself. Would that be okay?"

"Sure. What do you want to know?" Rachel noticed that she looked directly at her when she asked the question. This was nothing new to her; when they questioned a recently traumatized female, they typically seemed to gravitate to her. She'd heard the same thing from other female agents.

"Well, Detective Branson tells us that Edwin had been having a rough time lately. Could you tell us a bit about that?"

"He lost his job two months ago," she said, starting right away. She spoke as if it were of no great consequence to her. She spoke with the same inflection and emotion she might use while describing a recent trip to the grocery store. It led Rachel to believe that she had yet to completely accept her husband's death, that her brain was still trying to process it all. "We'd done a good job of saving over the years, so we were okay. And we'd be okay for about a year or so. He started putting

28

his resume out there and going on interviews right away but there wasn't much out there. The few jobs he did get callbacks on would have resulted in massive pay cuts and, though I know it sounds a little pretentious, he would have been *far* too qualified for these jobs."

"What did he do for a living?" Jack asked.

"He was a copywriter for a marketing firm. Mostly digital projects."

"What was his state of mind like before the layoff?" Rachel asked.

"Not the best. Edwin had always suffered from depression for as long as I knew him. He'd never been hospitalized for it or anything, but he was on meds. They worked most of the time but there would be a few days out of every month or so where he just had this sort of gray cloud around him."

"But it didn't affect his day-to-day life?"

"No, not at all," Hannah said. She chewed on a strawberry for a moment and then added: "But still, when I got the call and they later ruled it was a suicide by jumping off the bridge, there was a part of me that really wasn't all the surprised. I know that sounds awful, but...I didn't realize until I got the news that there was a small part of me that had almost *expected* it to happen sooner or later."

It was a strange comment, but Rachel had to remind herself that it was coming from a woman who seemed not to have accepted the reality of the situation yet. It also made her feel terrible for the woman. What must it be like to see a loved one suffering so badly from depression, but feeling helpless to do anything about it?

"Did he ever talk to you about the way he was feeling on the bad days?"

"We used to talk about it, sure." She pushed her bowl of oatmeal softly away, either having had her fill or too focused on the conversation at hand to properly eat. "But for the last year and a half or so, not so much. I didn't mind, though. He'd started going to support groups about it."

"Support groups for depression or suicidal thoughts?" Jack asked.

"You know, as bad as it sounds, I don't quite know. At the risk of sounding heartless, I assume the topic of suicide is going to come up in support groups about depression. So I'd assume it came up here and there."

"Did he ever mention it to you?" Rachel asked. "Was there ever any indication of him wanting to commit suicide?"

"I've been wondering the same thing," Hannah said. "I've been going back over and over it all in my mind—every conversation. But I swear, I can't think of a single time he ever mentioned wanting to take his own life. Not even on his worst days."

"How about the days leading up to it?" Jack asked. "What sort of mood was he in?"

"That's just the thing. He seemed to be in a pretty good mood. He'd even mentioned maybe taking a weekend trip up to Maine next month. Nothing seemed off, but then again there were times when I couldn't even tell when he was depressed until after the fact. So…as far as I know, he was in a decent mood in his last days."

"Do you happen to know the name of the support group he was part of?" Rachel asked. "Or perhaps the person that leads it?"

"I already have that information," Branson said.

"Just one last thing, Mrs. Newkirk," Rachel said, almost apologetically." I'm sure you heard about the eyewitness account about the possibility of a second person on the scene, correct?"

Hannah nodded, plucking aimlessly at her bowl of fruit.

"Do you know of anyone from those meetings that Edwin might have struck up a friendship with? Or, on the other hand, anyone he might have upset in any way?"

"I simply don't know," she said. "He kept a lot of what they talked about at group to himself. If he made friends or enemies there, I never heard about them."

Branson looked to Rachel and Jack, giving them a look that seemed to ask: *Are we good here?* Rachel thought they were. With no deeper insights into what her husband might have been thinking in the moments leading up to his apparent suicide, there wasn't much else to get out of her.

"Thanks for your time, Mrs. Newkirk," she said. "If you happen to think of anything of note, please let us know."

"You can contact me directly," Branson said.

Hannah nodded and waved to them, but did not get up. She stared forlornly at her two bowls, one with oatmeal, the other with fruit. Rachel felt terrible for the woman. She'd seen this sort of detachment before and knew that it was likely to end in a total meltdown where the grief and sense of loss came spilling out of her like a flood.

They left the apartment and reconvened in the street. "You said you have the information on the support group?" Rachel asked Branson.

"I do. I can text it to you, if you like. It's just the name of the group and the woman that heads it up."

"That's a good place to start, I suppose."

"What about the other families?" Jack asked. "Have you had the chance to speak with the families of the other two jumpers?"

"I've spoken with the wife of the first jumper on the phone, but very briefly. She's open to meeting, but I honestly haven't gotten to her yet."

"Can we take that from you, then?" Rachel asked.

"Absolutely. It was my understanding you guys would be taking this off of my hands, anyway. I'm happy to pitch in, but I already have a new homicide case on my desk when I get back to the station."

"That's fine," Rachel said. "We'll run it, if you'll just send anything you have aside from the police and coroner's reports we've already seen."

"Sounds good. I can have it all to you within the hour. For now, I can get you started on the family of the first victim. It's about a twenty-minute ride away from here, in Manhattan. I'll call ahead to let them know you're coming."

It was a relief to Rachel. In fact, it felt like a head start. And as they parted ways—Branson heading for his car while Rachel and Jack took up their rental—Rachel tried to think of a man hiding his depression from his wife. Yes, Hannah had been aware of Edwin's depression, but surely he hadn't told her everything. It made her think what Edwin may have been hiding. She felt it was a stretch to just assume a suicidal man might have been hiding secrets, but then again…she knew quite a bit about hiding dark, secret things.

***

The first jumper had been forty-two-year-old Joseph Staunton. The police report told the very simple story of his death, that he jumped from the Manhattan Bridge, likely from the north subway tracks on the lower deck. His body had been found in the water, but the state of his body suggested that he struck the ground just shy of the river on the Manhattan side. No one saw him jump, but his body was discovered by an NYPD officer on routine patrol, just happening to catch a glimpse of Staunton's orange shirt bobbing in the water.

Rachel tried to keep all of this in mind as she parked the rental in front of the Stauntons' rather expensive home in a small strip of suburban Manhattan. Joseph Staunton had left behind a wife, Ellen, and two children, one of whom had started their freshman year of college in Boston a month ago. Even with just these few details it felt different than it had when visiting Hannah Newkirk. With the Newkirks, there was at least some doubt as to whether or not Edwin had actually jumped. But with Joseph Staunton, everything in the report seemed to point toward an uncontested suicide. She had a feeling the mood in the Staunton home would be vastly different than what they had experienced with Hannah Newkirk.

She was proven right almost the instant the door was opened. It was answered by an older woman with a birdlike face. She regarded them warmly as she ushered them inside. "Thanks so much for coming," she said. "I'm Pam, Ellen's mother. She received the call from Detective Branson, saying you were on the way. She *wants* to speak with you, but I'm afraid she's a mess. I've told her I'll sit with her as she speaks with you, if that's okay?"

"That's perfectly fine," Rachel said. They then ran through quick introductions before entering further into the house. While Pam did not bother with any further introductions, there were several other family members present. Rachel saw a grieving young man sitting in the den, his head in his hands as an older man seemed to pray over him. Two others sat in the same room, all quiet and gloomy.

Pam led them by the den, down a hallway with hardwood floors. The walls boasted several pictures of the family: graduation pictures, vacation pictures, group family photos done by a professional. Near the end of the hallway, they came to a large room on the left. The built-in bookcases and the large oak desk near the back made Rachel assume it was an office or study of some kind. A small loveseat sat against the far wall, facing the desk. There was a woman half-sitting, half-lying on the loveseat. She looked to be in her early forties and incredibly tired. Her hair looked greasy and the bags under her eyes made Rachel feel tired simply looking at them.

"Ellen," Pam said. "The FBI agents are here to speak with you."

The woman turned her head slowly and it seemed to take her a full three seconds to even acknowledge the fact that she had visitors.

"Oh, thank you," she said. Her voice was soft, though not because she was whispering There was a hoarse and almost gravelly nature to it. Rachel imagined the poor woman had been howling and screaming over the loss of her husband for the last few days. "I appreciate you coming," she went on, "but I'm afraid you're wasting your time. There's no real crime around it from what I can tell. He jumped. He…killed himself." The last two words came out with an undertone of anger on them.

"We're in town because there have been some similar incidents lately," Rachel said.

Something like confusion spread across Ellen's face for a moment. "You think they might be connected somehow?"

"We just don't know. That's what we're trying to find out."

"How many others?"

"Two," Jack said. "Including your husband's, it's been one a night for the last three days."

"I hate to ask such personal questions," Rachel said, "but what was Joseph's demeanor like over the last few days?"

"He seemed perfectly fine. As I told Detective Branson, Joe used to deal with depression. It got pretty severe for a while, but he started taking medicine and seeing a therapist. It took a while, but he turned a corner. I mean…there were days where he was like a different person altogether. Now, given what's happened, I can't help but wonder if he was faking it. But…"

She stopped here and started to weep softly. She turned her head away, looking out the window as she tried to get herself under control.

"She's right," Pam said from the doorway. "I saw it, too. He was like a changed man. If he was playing a part or just acting, he had everyone fooled."

"He wasn't acting," Ellen said, now sounding quite confident. "He was better. His doctor said so, the therapist discharged him, and he stopped going to the support group he sometimes attended. He was *happy*."

Another support group, Rachel thought. Little alarm bells started to chime in her head.

"Did anything happen over the last few weeks or so that may have upset him?" Jack asked.

"Nothing here at home," Ellen said. "If there was anything, like with work or friends, he never told me."

"What did he do for work?" Rachel asked.

"He was a developmental programmer for a few different software companies. He worked some very long days every now and then, but it was always form home. And he loved his job, so the long days never bothered him. I don't think his reason for…for doing what he did stemmed from work."

"You mentioned a support group," Rachel said. "Would you happen to know the leader? Maybe the name of it?"

"I'm not sure of the name. But the leader is a woman named Becky Height. She called to ask if she could do anything for me. She's a real sweetheart from what I can tell."

Rachel noted the name and tucked it away in her head. She looked back at the doorway to Pam and saw the signs of a concerned mother. She wanted them out, but was being too polite to say so. As far as they were concerned, Joseph's death was a suicide and their being here was only drawing things out. Rachel agreed with this sentiment and now that they had a name to go on, she thought they'd gotten more than enough.

"We'll leave you alone now," Rachel said. "Thanks for your time and truly…we're sorry for your loss."

They headed back outside and Rachel found herself having to work a little more than usual to shrug off the feeling of despair and sadness she'd felt in the house. As she made her way to the car, she saw Jack tapping at his phone.

"Got that email from Branson," he said. "What did Ellen say the name of the support group leader is?"

"Becky Height."

Even before Jack had a chance to confirm it, Rachel knew what he was about to say. He held up his phone and nodded. "She just happens to be the leader of the support group Edwin Newkirk belonged to, also."

"Got a number?"

"And an address," he said as he got into the car, already plugging Becky Height's address into his phone.

CHAPTER EIGHT

One of the things Jack Rivers had been noticing more and more over the past five years or so was that the number of people working from home was increasing by staggering numbers with the passing of each year. There was no real reason for a fifty-year-old woman to be at home just before one o'clock on a Friday afternoon, but Becky Height was. She seemed supremely irritated when she came to the door, but she was home all the same.

"Can I ask what this is in reference to?" she asked sternly after seeing the badges of the two FBI agents standing outside the door of her Manhattan apartment.

"We're looking into the deaths of two men from your depression support group," Rachel said. "Joseph Staunton and Edwin Newkirk."

"Oh, I see," Becky said, the irritation dwindling the smallest bit. "Come in, come in, but wait in the kitchen, please. I'm finishing up a call." She pointed to the very thin headset on her head—so small and nondescript that Jack hadn't noticed it right away. "I have it on mute, and I'll be done at one o'clock."

It felt a bit odd to take orders from a woman they'd just met, especially a woman they had come to question, but one o'clock was only five minutes away and he didn't see the point in arguing. Rachel seemed fine with it as well, entering through the opened door with a quick nod and a smile.

Becky didn't even bother leading them to the kitchen. She simply walked out of the foyer and down a hall, where she then pointed them in the direction of the kitchen while she disappeared into a large room, shutting the door behind her. Jack and Rachel walked into the small but very quaint kitchen. It was a basic L shape with a small island in the center of the room. Afternoon sunlight came in through a window over the sink.

"You ever been bossed around by someone you're looking to question?" Jack asked.

Rachel seemed to be studying the marble counters when she gave a half-hearted chuckle. "No. But I'm assuming she works from home as a therapist or counselor."

"How do you know that?"

"I don't. I'm assuming. If she leads support groups for people with depression and works from home in a job that requires her to speak with people on the phone, I'd guess it's for some sort of telehealth."

Jack nodded, impressed with how quickly she was able to make those connections. She'd always been very good at it. But as she continued to look passively around the kitchen, Jack couldn't help but notice that something still seemed a little disconnected about Rachel. While he certainly felt for her in regards to the news about her grandmother, he still couldn't help but feel that something deeper was going on. He'd felt it several weeks ago when they had worked a case together; when he'd called it out or tried to get her to talk about it, she'd gotten defensive and uncharacteristically hostile. He thought he still sensed traces of it now but he had no idea how to broach it again without pushing her further away.

As he wrestled with this, Becky Height finally came walking into the kitchen. She looked hurried and a little embarrassed as she went to the fridge and got out a bottle of spring water. "Either of you want one?" she asked.

They both declined as Becky unscrewed the top of her water. She sighed and looked to both of them as she took her first sip. When it was down, she said: "So, the FBI is looking into Joseph's and Edwin's suicides?"

"That's right," Jack said. "There's just enough evidence behind Edwin Newkirk's jump to suggest it may not have been an intentional act."

"And what about Joseph?"

"We don't know just yet," Rachel said. "But there have been three in just as many days and if one of them seems to suggest some sort of foul play, they all need to be researched and investigated as such, just to make sure."

"There was another man," Jack said. "The second of what is now three apparent suicides. The second was a man named Nicholas Harding. Does that name ring a bell? Has he been in any of your groups?"

Becky thought about it for a moment and slowly started to shake her head. "No, I don't believe so. You do have to keep in mind, though, that sometimes people will give a fake name. It doesn't happen often, believe it or not, but there *is* always that chance. Now…other than that basic information, what, exactly, do you need from me?"

"First of all, how did you know about Edwin Newkirk's suicide?" Rachel asked.

"The police called me. My business card was in his wallet."

"Were you surprised to hear it had happened?"

"I was. Edwin was often a voice of encouragement in our meetings. Sure, he was dealing with his own things, but he seemed to always find a way to speak some sort of brightness into other people. I spoke with him several times about how sometimes it isn't exactly healthy to bury your own grief and feelings just to help others, but it's just what he did." She considered something for a moment and shook her head. "No, I would have never thought he'd do this. Not Edwin."

"And what about Joseph Staunton?" Rachel asked.

"Joseph is a different story. There were a few times over the past year or so where I seriously considered referring him to the mental health ward over at the hospital. He was a quiet man, very inside of himself, you know? If I'm being honest—and this is awful to say—but I was not really very surprised when I learned about Joseph. He had a network of people to help and meds that I'm not sure he was taking regularly. But…in the end, he made the ultimate decision, I suppose."

"How often has this happened to you?" Jack asked. "How many times have you been informed that someone from one of your groups had taken their own life?"

"Far too often. I've been leading these sort of groups for nearly ten years now. There are victories for sure, but moments like these make those victories seem small. This *is* the first time I've ever had two members of a group take their lives within such a small amount of time, though."

"So you'd say this whole situation with three jumpers in such a short time is uncommon?" Rachel asked.

"Not necessarily. People that come to groups like mine or to therapists are obviously looking to improve. In those cases, yes, I'd say it's a little strange. But as I'm sure you can imagine, suicides aren't all that uncommon, especially in places as large as New York City. Somehow, though, it has remained very low in the nation's average for suicides over the past five years or so."

"Our next obvious step in all of this is to find out *who* might have been involved if there was indeed a third party. Can you think of anyone in this same group that might have had something against Joseph and Edwin? Maybe anyone that might have wanted to hurt them—or anyone else at all, for that matter?"

Becky sipped from her water again. Jack was pretty sure she was simply stalling this time. When she was done, a frown crept along her mouth. "Even if I thought there might be such a threat in the group, I can't give you that sort of information. As I'm sure you know, it's very private."

"We understand and appreciate that," Rachel said. "But if there is indeed someone facilitating all of this, there's a very good chance they could hurt someone tonight. So far, we're talking about one victim a night for the last three nights."

"With all due respect," Jack added, "would you rather give us a potential name now or wake up tomorrow morning to find that there's been a fourth—that there probably *is* someone behind all of this and you could have helped prevent the death of the fourth victim?"

The bluntness of the comment seemed to shock Becky momentarily. Her face scrunched up a bit and it was clear that she had not appreciated his comment. Still, Jack could tell she was going to give a name. She could see it in the slight sadness in her eyes—a sadness that started to look more like guilt the longer she did not speak.

"I thought of this myself just last night and a bit this morning," she finally answered. "About five or six months ago, there was this one man that came to the meetings. He came off and on, a week here and a week there, never anything consistent. He was clearly depressed but there were some other mental issues there, too. He stopped coming to the meetings altogether when I recommended he see a therapist or maybe even go to the hospital. The thing with him, though, was that he'd sometimes sort of poke fun at the problems other people were having. And that caused some issues. There was one night as I was leaving, I caught him and Edwin having words in the parking lot. I had no delusion that it would break into a fight, but there was a lot of shouting and name-calling."

"Was that the only time anything like that happened between them?" Jack asked.

"Of that magnitude, yes. But there were instances here and there during the meetings where this other man would get antagonistic towards him."

"And what about Joseph Staunton?" Rachel asked. "Did he ever have any interactions with this man?"

"No. I don't believe so. I can't even recall if they were ever in a meeting together. If you like, I can see if I can find my attendance sheets to confirm."

"What is this man's name?" Rachel asked.

It was obvious that Becky did not want to give the name, but she did so without much hesitation all the same. "Ronald Welch."

"And you said it's been five or six months since you've seen him?"

"Yes, give a week or two."

"Do you by any chance have a phone number or address?"

"No."

"Can you guess his age, perhaps?"

"He was forty-five. I know because he complained about how he thought his life would have been this picture of success and wealth by the time he was forty and now that he was five years past it, everything seemed to be getting worse. He——"

Becky paused here as a buzzing noise interrupted her. She took her phone out of her pocket, checked the display, and looked to them with a sense of urgency. "This is my next call. I have to take it. I work for a telehealth firm dealing with mental health and my clients are——"

"It's quite all right," Rachel said. "You've been more than accommodating. We can see ourselves out."

Jack thought they could have gotten a bit more from the conversation and maybe Becky could have put the call off for another few minutes. Rather than argue this, he simply followed Rachel out of the kitchen as Becky hurried back to the large room she'd disappeared into earlier—presumably her office.

When they were back out on the porch, Jack finally said something. "You really think we got all we could out of her?"

"I do. She hated giving us that name, but she did. So she had no reason to keep anything else from us. I think she told us all she could."

Jack supposed this made sense, but still…there was something about the abruptness of the decision that seemed very *un*-Rachel. She'd done a few things here and there over the last few weeks that had been similar to this and he chalked it up to whatever was going on in her life that she was choosing not to tell him about.

"Besides," she said as they neared the car. "We learned the most important thing."

"Yeah, we did get a name."

"No, not the name. I mean the fact that I guessed it perfectly. She's doing mental health through a telehealth system."

With a snarky and playful smile that was very much in line with Rachel's typical personality, she got into the car. As Jack did the same, he could not shake the feeling that despite the occasional flash of normalcy, there was something truly wrong with his partner.

And he was going to find out what it was.

CHAPTER NINE

Rachel placed a call to Branson and asked him to run a search for a man named Ronald Welch, assumed to be either forty-five or forty-six years of age. He called back seven minutes later with two hits. One was an employee with a small yet successful law firm. The other seemed to be unemployed and was drawing disability. Though the records on file did not specify the disability, Rachel was quite sure this would be the Ronald Welch they were looking for. It seemed to her that a man drawing disability would run a much larger chance of suffering from depression than someone working at a successful law firm.

With Ronald Welch's address plugged into Jack's GPS, they headed into the East Side. Welch's apartment was on the first floor of an apartment building that had the sort of exterior that was easy to pass by without even realizing it was there. Crammed between another apartment building and a currently vacant storefront, the front of the building was featureless aside from its windows. Rachel and Jack had the good fortune of climbing the stairs just as an older lady was coming out, so they didn't have to be buzzed in.

They made their way through the lobby, which looked to have been recently mopped but still somehow smelled of old shoes and faint body odor. They followed the hallway down to Ronald Welch's apartment, number 121, and knocked on the door. Rachel could hear a television through the door, the channel tuned to something that had a bit of overdramatic music playing in the background. Given that it was now officially afternoon, she wondered if Ronald Welch might be a fan of daytime soap operas.

She heard an annoyed grunt from inside the apartment and then the squeaking of springs as someone pushed themselves out of a chair. Several moments later, the door was answered, opening only a few inches before coming to a stop thanks to the chain lock up top. A man with a pudgy face peered through the crack, a single blue eye staring out at them.

"Yeah? Who's it?"

"Are you Mr. Ronald Welch?" Jack asked.

"Might be. Who are *you*?"

Jack and Rachel both showed their badges, but Jack continued to do the talking. "Agents Rivers and Gift, FBI. We're investigating a few recent deaths and are looking for anyone who might be able to offer insights into them. As we've been digging into it, your name came up."

"My name? About deaths?" Welch seemed genuinely confused and surprised. "Who gave you my name?"

"If you'd allow us to come inside, we could discuss it at length," Rachel said.

She saw a slight flicker of embarrassment in Welch's one eye that she could see. "Er, well, I don't usually have company. I'd be real ashamed for you to come in and see the place like this. Is it okay if we just talk out there in the hallway?"

"That will be fine," Jack said. Rachel knew that for now, yes, it was fine. But if they suspected him beyond this line of questioning, they'd have to end up getting into his apartment. She was always on high alert when people refused to allow them into their homes. She knew it didn't always point to the fact that something was being hidden, but it was a feeling that came up in all those situations regardless.

Welch opened the door the rest of the way and joined them in the hall. He was a hefty man, for sure; doctors would easily label him as obese, and it made Rachel wonder if his weight had something to do with his disability, or the other way around. His hair was slightly greasy and he had the overall look of a man who didn't really get out much.

"So, am I allowed to ask who died?" he asked.

"Three have died in the past three days," Rachel said. "They all appear to be suicides, with the exception of one. We found out earlier today that two of them attended a depression support group that you once attended. The organizer of that group says that you had a few choice words with one of the men."

"My God," Welch said. "They…wait…which ones? Are you talking about the fella that was griping about the medicine he was taking?"

"We don't know the extent of the discussions, but we do know that you were quite confrontational with him. Do you recall the exchange you had with a man from the group out in a parking lot?"

"I do, for sure." He nodded his head solemnly and looked at them with confusion in his eyes. "I just…God, I don't even remember his name."

Rachel wasn't quite sure if she believed this or not. She searched his face for any tells—narrowing of the eyes, nervously twitching mouth, gaze shifting all over the place—but saw nothing of the sort.

"Mr. Welch, do you remember what the two of you were arguing about?" Jack asked.

"Nothing worth arguing about. And you know…I hate to say it, but it was my fault. I know it hasn't been all that long ago, but I was a very different person back then. Sort of an asshole. If I remember right, he was just going on and on about how his problems were stupid compared to what I was going through. Like I said…sort of an asshole."

Rachel thought she saw some hesitation in the way he said this. It was almost as if he regretted calling the man an asshole, given the nature of the case. Maybe he was telling the truth after all.

"What *were* you going through?" Jack asked.

"I'd just had a stroke and was dealing with diabetes. I had just officially filed for disability and hated it. I felt like a failure. A lot of self-loathing, you know? I took it out on others before I decided to actually try doing something about it." He chuckled nervously here and patted his stomach. "Believe it or not, what you see here is an improvement. I've dropped forty pounds in the last five months."

Rachel could see the embarrassment and loathing in Welch's eyes as he spoke to them. While she'd never been one to trust someone's story based on simple facial expressions, she did find that she believed him. Not only that, but as bad as it made her feel, she found it difficult to imagine someone of Ronald Welch's size climbing out to the edge of the suicide rails on the Williamsburg Bridge. It would be far from impossible, sure, but very unlikely.

"Mr. Welch, would you be able to provide proof of your whereabouts over the past three nights if asked to do so?"

"Probably. Well, I mean, for the first two nights, I was here most of the night. But there's plenty of online history to support that, I guess."

"What about last night?" Jack asked.

"I was down at Delancey Gym. I go late because I don't like the stares during normal hours."

"How long were you there?"

"Until midnight, when they closed. After that, I went by the grocery store for some eggs and milk. I don't have receipts or anything, but I used my credit card so I guess there's a trail, right?"

"Right," Rachel said. "And if it does come to that, we may ask to get access to the credit card report and maybe even speak with the gym."

"Sure." Welch seemed uncomfortable with the situation, but there was sadness to his voice and face rather than fear or guilt. "I guess this is another of those instances where you look back on the person you used to be and sort of…well, sort of wish you could change a few things."

"We've all been there, Mr. Welch," Jack said in a tone that indicated he truly believed this. Jack Rivers had never been much of a bullshitter. "Thanks for your time."

They turned back toward the lobby, and Rachel heard Ronald Welch's door close behind them. When they came to the front doors, Jack echoed a private thought Rachel had inside.

"No way in hell did he sneak around in the dark, go out on the edge of that bridge, and push Edwin Newkirk."

"I was thinking the same thing," Rachel said. "And he gave us some pretty credible paths to look down with the gym and his credit card use at the grocery store."

"So we're back to having no leads."

"Seems that way. But I think we should reach out to Branson again. I'd like to have a look at the phone records of all three of the victims if they've been pulled. The idea we were chasing with Welch seems to have something to it, don't you think?"

"You mean someone antagonizing the jumpers and pushing them to jump?"

"Yeah, especially with Edwin Newkirk. Everyone seems so surprised he would have done it."

"I'll reach out to Branson while you drive."

"Drive where?"

"To the Manhattan Bridge, to get a look at where Joseph Staunton died. And from there, the bridge the second victim jumped from—the Ramble Bridge in Cold Spring."

It was a good enough plan for now, so Rachel got behind the wheel and started driving to Manhattan while Jack made the call to Branson. And with the afternoon winding down, she could not help but feel that they were racing against a clock. If there was indeed a killer behind these three deaths, he'd been working at night. And Rachel saw no reason he'd change up his plans on the fly. With nightfall just five hours away, that clock ticked louder and louder and Rachel had to fight quite hard not to feel the imagined sound was also an indicator of her own recently shortened life.

CHAPTER TEN

Walking along the pedestrian footpath on the side of the bridge and looking down below, it's easy to imagine someone falling. The space between the rail and the river and ground below practically seems to call out for someone or something to come and fill that space. The rush of wind by a body, slipping past the ears and blowing hair aside...it has to be almost peaceful for a moment, right?

A thin smile crosses their face at the thought.

A few joggers and a bicyclist pass by but never even notice. Not the smile, not the way their hands are stuffed into their pockets, not the way their eyes look over the rail, wondering if the fall would be enough to kill someone. There's no real science to it. The victims fall and, if the drop is bad enough, they die. So far, they'd all died. And at least one of the bridges had been closer to the ground than this one. This one would do fine.

A woman walking a small lapdog came walking briskly by. The dog was quite interested in the individual walking slowly down the walkway, occasionally peering over the side of the bridge. It came to a stop at their shoe and pawed playfully at it.

"Jewel!" the owner cried. "Leave the poor person alone, would you?"

They smiled, leaning down to pet Jewel between her shaggy little head. "Oh, it's okay. She's adorable."

"She's a spoiled mess is what she is!"

Giving one more little scratch on the head, they looked up to Jewel's owner. She looked to be in her early fifties. She was wearing a sun visor, a T-shirt with a generic slogan on it, and shorts that no women over thirty should ever wear. It would have been a great deal of fun to throw her ass over the bridge. Then they'd have their answer. Then they'd know if this drop was high enough.

Of course, they couldn't do that. There were too many people running, walking, riding their bikes. And all of them were doing those things, separated from a free fall to their death by just a foot or so, and one single steel rail. The thought of it made them a little giddy—it wasn't a sexual excitement or even anything related to anxiousness. It was like being a kid again and standing in line for the best roller coaster at the park.

It would happen tonight. They did not need Jewel's owner. They knew it would work and exactly how it needed to be done.

Jewel and her owner walked away from the stranger. Totally unremarkable and plain in just about every way, no one would have suspected them. It was almost too perfect. The smile remained on the plain face, the unremarkable and unrememberable face, as they reached the other end of the bridge. It was even wider now, as they could easily imagine that final moment before gravity took the next victim. There was that moment of abject terror in the eyes, the drawing in of breath that almost never came out in their frozen terror.

They clenched their hands in their pockets, palms slick with sweat.

Tonight could not get here fast enough.

CHAPTER ELEVEN

A quick survey of the Manhattan Bridge showed Rachel and Jack absolutely nothing. The suicide prevention measures on this bridge were slightly better than the ones on the Williamsburg Bridge, though not by much. There was a safety fence that was built along the very edge of the bridge in a way that was aesthetically subtle to the casual viewer, though making it harder or any jumpers to get to the East River. There had been no obvious signs of where the fence had been cut or torn through, though there were a few spots that showed where attempts had been made to do so. Of course, there was simply no way to tell for sure if anyone had ever scaled it and gone to the other side.

Not that it really mattered, as Joseph Staunton had jumped just slightly away from the river.

As Rachel and Jack headed back to their car, Rachel thought that a quick check to see how many suicides had occurred from the bridge might answer that question for her.

They were coming off of the bridge when Rachel's phone rang. She assumed it would be Branson, hopefully with a good news update, informing them that he'd have those phone records to them shortly. The caller ID told her that it wasn't Branson, as it was a Virginia area code. She nearly let the call go to voicemail, as she did not recognize the number. But with all of her health concerns, a young daughter in a public school, and a husband who was often preoccupied with work, it was hard to ignore it completely.

"Excuse me a second, would you?" she said to Jack. He nodded and continued on toward the car as she took the call.

"This is Agent Gift."

"Hello there, Agent," a slightly raspy male voice said. "Are you out catching bad guys?"

"Who is this?"

"If that *is* what you're doing, I thought I could call to offer my help. Maybe it would save you another trip."

Even before the last part of the comment, Rachel knew who it was. Her blood went cold as she realized that Alex Lynch was on the other end of the phone. The very same Alex Lynch that she'd relied on to help with her last case and had somehow been able to decipher that she

47

was sick. With him on the other end of the line, Rachel wasn't sure which she was more upset about: his past grisly crimes, or that he knew her secret.

"How the hell did you get my number?"

"I think I'll keep that as my little secret for right now, if you don't mind."

Her mind whirled with what this could mean. If he had her number *and* access to a phone, it could be bad. He knew her secret, after all. She had no idea how he'd known, but the fact remained that he *did know*. He'd somehow sensed it on her and when he'd called it out, she hadn't denied it.

"Nothing to say?" Alex asked from the other end.

"Why are you calling me?"

"Just checking in, friend to friend." He snickered here, a muddy and unpleasant sound. "Nothing wrong with that, now is there?"

"I'm not your friend," she spat. "Get that out of your head right now."

"That's a shame. Because I thought friends kept secrets. And since I'm sitting on this pretty big secret of yours, I thought that meant we were friends. If you don't want to be friends, Agent Gift, I just don't know what I might do with this secret I have."

She gripped her phone tighter, looking back to the bridge. Again, she found herself wondering what it might be like to jump, to give her life to gravity and not have to worry about her secret. God, it would all be so easy.

"If we're such good friends," Rachel said, trying to keep the anger out of her voice, "then why don't you start by telling me why you're calling."

"Oh, nothing really. Just to screw with your head. Just to remind you that I'm here and I know." He laughed here, a soft throaty noise that made her cringe. "You go catch those bad guys, Agent Gift. And if you ever need my assistance again, you know where to find me."

The line went dead before she could say anything else. Rachel didn't move for a moment. In fact, she found it hard to breathe. She was afraid a single breath would cause her to expel a scream or a bout of weeping. Her entire body seemed to lock up for a moment as a chill of despair crept through her.

What the hell were you thinking going to that madman for help? she asked herself.

Rather than try to come up with an answer, she uttered a silent curse and pocketed her phone. She took a moment to collect herself.

Her hands were trembling slightly and she felt like she might be on the verge of a panic attack. She allowed herself time enough to take a few deep, calming breaths, trying to figure out what to do about this. Should she contact the prison and tell them to monitor his calls, to make sure the maniac never called her again? That seemed like a bit much. Though, if he called again, it might be an avenue she'd pursue.

When her hands were no longer shaking, Rachel hurried down to catch up with Jack where he'd parked their car just off of Chrystie Street. As she crossed the road and joined him, she saw that he was standing against the side of the car, reading something on his phone.

He barely glanced up at her, his eyes still mostly on his phone. "Everything okay?"

"Yeah," she said, hoping it was convincing. "How about you? Reading something interesting?"

"Yes, actually. Branson sent the phone records over for all three of the potential victims."

"Potential?"

"Yeah. I'm not calling them victims until we know for sure there's foul play here. I mean, so far it all looks like suicides to me. And if it quacks like a duck and looks like a duck…it's a well, in this case, I guess it's a duck that killed itself."

"That's not quite how the saying goes."

He ignored her, still looking at the screen. "I *will* say, though, that these phone records do look sort of fishy. You got your laptop?"

"Yeah, it's in my bag."

Rachel unlocked the trunk and took her laptop out of the one bag she'd packed for the trip. As she powered it up and got into the car, Jack forwarded the records to her email. By the time he got into the passenger seat, the laptop was powered up. He took it from her without asking and she raised her eyebrows at him. "Excuse me…"

"We can look it over right over there, at that pizza place. I'd like to eat at some point today."

Rachel realized that she also hadn't eaten anything since the little dry pastry the airline had provided. "That's not a bad idea," she said, reaching back out to snatch up her laptop.

They locked up the car and walked the block over to the pizzeria Jack had spotted. They were seated quickly and as they waited for their order to come out, they looked over the phone records.

"So the first thing I noticed while trying to compare them all on my phone," Jack said, "is that each of them had a series of calls from private numbers in the day or two leading up to their deaths. Of course, we can't tell from these records if the calls were from the same number or different numbers."

"So we need to contact the cell providers and get someone else at the bureau on it." Rachel sighed as she said this. She'd been down that particular road before. Cell providers were often notoriously slow in getting information like that. Even if they called it in right now, it might be twenty-four to forty-eight hours before they got a result. Rather than get too disheartened by this, she pointed to the records. "And look, those calls all come between nine and midnight."

On her laptop screen, she had three windows open, each window showing one of the victims' records. Lined up in such a way, it was easy to make the comparisons. It also made it quite easy for Rachel to see another similarity in the records—one she felt might be even more pivotal than the calls from the private numbers.

"See this eight hundred number?" she asked, pointing first to Joseph Staunton's number. She then trailed her finger to the second victim's records, forty-nine year-old Nicholas Harding. The eight hundred number was there, too.

"Yeah, and they're both outgoing."

Rachel then scanned Edwin Newkirk's records and saw the same number. And the most interesting thing of all was that all three men had called the same eight hundred number on the night they'd allegedly decided to take their own lives.

Rachel took out her phone and instantly started tapping in the number. It rang three times before it was answered by a soft female voice.

"Better Days Prevention Hotline, New York. This is Samantha. Who am I talking to?"

"This is Special Agent Rachel Gift with the FBI. You said *prevention*. Is this a suicide prevention hotline?"

Samantha sounded very confused when she said, "Yes ma'am. And you're FBI?"

"I am. And I need to speak to your supervisor, please."

"Um, sure, yeah. One second. Hold please."

There was a little click and then peaceful-sounding ambient music came over the line. While she waited, she shrugged at Jack and said, "You may as well go ahead and see what you can do about getting the cell providers to get the actual numbers from those private calls. And while you're at it…maybe flag down the waitress. I get the feeling that we're going to need to get this pizza to go."

CHAPTER TWELVE

Through the supervisor, Rachel learned two very important things that she felt would help tremendously with the case. First, she learned that Better Days Prevention Hotline was a nationwide service with hubs set up in twenty-one locations across the nation. The New York hub received upwards of eighty calls a week. Secondly, Rachel was also given the physical address of the call center, and it was just twenty minutes away from where she and Jack had attempted to enjoy a pizza. Her hope was that they could speak with the operators who had taken the calls of the victims. If so, that would provide insights into their lives that maybe even family and loved ones would not be able to provide.

The center was on the fourth floor and an unsuspecting building near Yorkville, tucked in among several other buildings that looked exactly alike. When they arrived, each having quickly eaten two slices of pizza in the car on the way over, the supervisor was waiting for them in a small waiting area that also served as a lobby.

"Agents?" the woman said, greeting them at the door. "I'm Shelby Elder, the New York supervisor."

Rachel and Jack introduced themselves and after that, Shelby wasted no time. She instantly led them down a small hallway with just two rooms along it, one on each wall. She opened the door to the right and they walked in. She was a trim woman who, in an odd way, looked just about the same way she moved: thorough, to the point, and with no nonsense. As they passed through the doorway, Rachel looked to the end of the hall. It emptied into a large room that was divided by several cubicles. She could hear a phone ringing somewhere further off and she could not help but wonder if it was a call coming from someone on the verge of ending their own life. Something about it was haunting but she managed to shake it off as she entered the office. Shelby closed the door behind them and, perhaps because there were no seats for her visitors, she opted to stand rather than sit behind the desk.

"On the phone, you said there were records that showed three recently dead people had called here, yes?"

"That's right," Rachel said. "And there are a few things we were hoping you could help us with. First of all, if there are recordings of the calls, we'd like to hear them. Secondly, we'd like to see if you can find out which of your operators spoke to them."

"Well, the calls might be tricky. They *are* recorded but as I'm sure you can understand, I need to get the sign-off from the regional manager up in Boston. Given that the FBI is involved, that should not be a problem."

Rachel had expected as much, so this wasn't as big of a blow as it sounded. "And the operators?"

"That won't be an issue," she said. "Do you have the records on you?"

"We do."

"I just need the number the call came from and the time the call was placed." She finally made her way back behind her desk and sat down behind a laptop. As Rachel recited the number and gave the times the three different victims called, Shelby typed it all into her laptop. She worked quickly and efficiently; she was apparently not bothered that there were two FBI agents watching her work. As she stopped clicking around on her screen, though, her brow began to furrow and a strange look came over her face.

"Everything okay?" Rachel asked.

"I don't know. I'm not sure what the statistical chances of something like this happening might be…but it appears that all three of these men spoke to the exact same operator."

Rachel, who typically did not buy into coincidences, sat up a bit straighter. This felt like the biggest potential lead they'd had so far.

"How many operators do you have on staff?" Jack asked.

"Well, they're all either part-time or volunteers, mostly working in four- or six-hour shifts. But we have thirty-two that all rotate out. This woman is a volunteer who mostly works the later hours."

"Can you call her and get her to come in soon?"

"Well, she's actually here right now. She's filling in for another volunteer who called in sick."

Rachel felt the same stirring in her guts she usually felt when she was certain they'd found something significant. With thirty-two operators, the chances of those three men calling on three consecutive nights and getting the same operator seemed much more than coincidental. "We need you to call her in here, please."

Shelby nodded, but seemed very uneasy with the idea. "How about this? There's a small conference room on the other side of the cubicles. I'm going to buzz her and tell her to step in there to meet us. No sense in the other operators getting unwarranted gossip ammo."

"That's fine," Rachel said.

Shelby picked up the landline phone on her desk and tapped in a three-digit extension. Only two seconds passed before there was an answer. Rachel and Jack listened as Shelby said, "Lisa, could you meet with me in the conference room? Uh-huh. Yes, right now, please." She hung up and still looked uneasy. She had remained polite throughout the brief conversation; there was no bass or threatening tone to her voice.

"How long has she been volunteering here?" Jack asked.

"Nearly two years now. I've never had a single issue with her performance. Lisa is one of those people that just sort of gels with anyone she meets. You'll see what I mean in a bit. Actually, the conference room is right beside her cubicle, so we can go on now if you want."

The three of them left Shelby's office and walked through the collection of cubicles that served as the call center. They stayed by the wall as to give the operators their privacy and came to a small conference room on the other side of the room. It was warm and inviting, giving an instant feeling of calmness and peace. The lighting was very low and even the desk in the center of the room looked as if it were glowing in the lights. There were light colors everywhere, from the curtains to the carpet. A tranquil seaside painting hung on the wall, but one that actually invoked awe and wonder rather than a ten-dollar one purchased from a thrift store. Rachel saw it all as being a very planned and purposeful feature for a place where people were always speaking to depressed individuals.

The woman Shelby had identified as Lisa was sitting at the sizable desk in the center of the room. She looked to be in her late twenties, a very pretty woman at first glance. Her blue eyes and blonde hair seemed to glow in the softness of the room. She had an aura of peace about her, which Rachel assumed went a long way toward success when you helped with a suicide prevention hotline. And though her smile lit up her face, her eyes narrowed the slightest bit when she saw two strangers enter the room behind Shelby. Lisa did not ask questions, though, instead waiting for Shelby to explain everything. Shelby closed the door behind her and took the seat across from Lisa. Rachel took the one next to Shelby while Jack chose to stand.

Shelby took the lead in a way that made Rachel assume she was a good supervisor. She kept a friendly demeanor throughout, but there was something in her tone and cadence that made it clear that things were about to get serious.

"Lisa, these are agents from the FBI—Agents Rivers and Gift. They're looking into a string of deaths and need to ask you some questions."

"Me?" Lisa asked. The confusion on her face seemed genuine. There was a good deal of fear in her eyes, too.

"Yes," Jack said. "We're looking into the deaths of three men that all look to be suicides. But the most recent one gives us some reason to think there might have been outside influences."

Rachel placed her phone on the table and turned it toward Lisa. "These are phone records from each of the men. Each one shows that they each called the Better Days Prevention hotline within six hours of taking their lives. All of them jumped from a bridge—a different bridge for each man."

"Lisa, we've asked to speak to you," Shelby said, "because the call logs indicate they each spoke with you. Not only that, but it seems they all spoke to you not too many days outside of the night they decided to take their own lives."

Lisa nodded, but her right hand slowly went to her face to cover her mouth. "Oh my God," she said. "I can't...I don't even know..."

"Lisa," Rachel said, "do you recall speaking with anyone who indicated they were going to jump?" Before Lisa could answer, Rachel tried to gauge her reaction. She was clearly troubled. That much was genuine. But as of right now, Rachel wasn't sure she bought into the level of shock she was showing.

"Yes," Lisa said. She struggled to keep her voice level and soft. When she finally seemed to have some sort of control over it, it was a soft and reassuring voice that Rachel was certain would sound calming and gentle over a telephone line. "Last night and then two nights before that."

"And what about the one in between? His name was Nicholas Harding."

"I remember him, sure. But he never got specific about how he planned to do it."

"In each of the calls, do you feel you were able to talk the men down?"

"Yes, I did. I was...I mean, Shelby can get the calls for you, and you can hear them. The man last night even said how foolish he felt at the end of it all."

"How long did you speak with them?" Jack asked.

Shelby got to her feet before Lisa could answer. "Let me go ahead and call the Boston office for approval. Hopefully I can have access to the calls within the next ten minutes or so. Please forgive me ahead of time if they need to speak with you."

She then left the room quickly, leaving Rachel and Jack to speak with Lisa. With Shelby gone, Lisa seemed even more fearful. She eyed the agent suspiciously and Rachel thought she might start crying at any moment.

"Lisa, did either of the men truly frighten you when you spoke with them?" Rachel asked. "Did you think any of them would go through with it?"

"The second man, I thought for sure would. He said I'd helped to talk him down, but I wasn't so sure. When my shift was over, I called the number back for sort of a wellness check. There was no answer, so…God, I guess he did it."

"Did you ever reach out to the police out of concern?" Jack asked.

"No. We are trained to do everything we can to talk them down. The people that call…one of the things they often worry about even when they change their mind on the line is that someone will find out they made the call. So remaining anonymous is a big deal to them. If I earn their trust and then break it by calling the police, it creates a very bad situation. If I remember correctly, when I took the training to be a volunteer, we learned that less than five percent of calls to suicide prevention hotlines are ever escalated to the police."

"And you use the same script and tactics for each one?" Rachel asked.

"There's no script, just guidelines and bullet points. We have to try to sort of get to know them so to speak. And based on their urgency, their problems, and the way they interact with this, *that's* how we know the best way to offer support."

Rachel tried to think of something else to ask, but really, she thought any questions would be answered by listening to the calls. She could also tell that one wrong word was going to have Lisa crying and potentially harder to question.

Jack stepped closer to the table and said, "I appreciate what you do here. Especially as a volunteer with no pay. I can't imagine what you go through sometimes. Like with these three men…you tried convincing them that there was something to live for, right?"

"Yes, and I thought…I thought I'd done a good job…"

Before they could get any farther, the door opened and Shelby walked in. She was carrying her laptop and had a determined expression on her face. She was a woman on a mission, a vibe that Rachel appreciated.

"Mark your calendars," Shelby said as she resumed her seat. "I got permission to access the calls within two minutes of asking. I'm assuming it had something to do with the fact that we're looking at three bodies."

"And you have all three of them?" Jack asked.

"Yes. Lisa, can you think of any reason one call might be more important than the other?"

"Not right offhand, no."

"And I'm so sorry," Rachel said, "but I have to ask: if we're going to hear something on here that's going to paint you in a negative light, it's going to be much better for you if you tell us now." But even as she said this, her final suspicions of Lisa had pretty much shriveled away. She found it very difficult to imagine this woman trying to convince someone to kill themselves.

"No," she said in almost a whisper. "Nothing like that." She didn't seem to take offense to the notion, apparently understanding that they were just doing their job.

"Then could you please play them in order, from oldest to most recent?" Rachel asked.

Shelby nodded, made a few clicks on her trackpad, and Lisa's voice came through the laptop speakers. "Better Days Prevention Hotline, New York. This is Lisa. Who am I speaking to this evening?"

"My name's Joseph. Or just Joe."

It wasn't just hearing the voice of a dead man through those little laptop speakers that chilled Rachel; it was also recalling how his wife had called him Joe. She continued to listen, the four of them basically frozen in place as they listened to the call.

"Joe, what are you up to this evening?"

"Well, I'm thinking about heading over to the Manhattan Bridge and jumping."

"Can you tell me what makes you want to do that?"

There was a moment's pause, and then a few huffs of breath that Rachel thought were the sounds of someone holding back sobs. "Because I can't beat this...I can't get past this depression and I'm just so damned sick of it."

"How long have you been dealing with it?" Lisa asked.

They listened to the entirety of the call, all eleven minutes of it. Rachel was beyond impressed with the way Lisa maneuvered the conversation. She never told him flat out that he was making a mistake and, on more than one occasion, had Joseph Staunton talking about things other than his depression and suicide plans—namely his son and his wife. And even Rachel had to agree that when the call had ended, Lisa had done an excellent job. Joseph sounded almost embarrassed when they ended the call, thanking her profusely.

"Questions?" Shelby asked before starting the second call.

"No," Rachel said. "In fact, I'm amazed at how well you did, Lisa." When Lisa seemed to barely acknowledge the compliment, Rachel felt certain she knew how the other two calls were going to go.

However, when Shelby started the second call and they got deeper into Nicholas Harding's call, the entire feel of it was different. It was clear that Harding was in a very dark place. There was nothing rehearsed or attention-seeking about it. He was just hopeless and angry. Rachel pitied Lisa for having to listen to it.

Four minutes into the call, she could hear Lisa floundering, trying to redirect the conversation. But Harding seemed bent on venting to anyone that would listen. In Quantico, during training, most agents had been forced to listen to recorded stage negotiations or the ramblings of murderers just to get a feel for it. Nicholas Harding's session reminded her of those classes.

"The only person that is going to give a fuck if I die is the crew that has to clean it up—be that the cops, some city worker, whoever. This has been a long time coming and I'm sort of pissed with myself that I haven't done it already."

"Well, surely there's *some* reason for not doing it if you feel so strongly about it," Lisa's voice responded. "Maybe deep down you know there's a reason you want to still be here."

"Oh sure, there's a reason. I'm a coward. It's one of the few things I *am* certain about."

The conversation went on for fifteen more minutes. The last thirty seconds were tense and it still baffled Rachel that the police weren't called. She understood the point of protocols but sometimes she also felt they needed to be pushed aside for the well-being of others.

"Nick, are you sure there isn't someone you can call?" Lisa asked. "Maybe someone you can speak with face-to-face?"

"There's no one. Anyone that would have spoken to me a year or so ago has turned their backs on me. I know I deserve it. I've ruined every relationship and everything else I touch. I just…Jesus, this is pointless."

"Nick, if you just—"

"Don't worry…Lisa, was it? I think I've talked about it just enough to back out for the fifth or sixth time. Thanks for taking the call."

"Nick, you know if you—"

But Harding ended the call. There was silence in the room, as if the call had taken place right there and then and they had all been hung up on. Rachel saw a few tears rolling down Lisa's face and she almost wanted to speak up and excuse the woman.

With slow hands, Shelby started playing the third call, the call that had come last night from Edwin Newkirk. Rachel noticed that Lisa looked on edge the entire time. It was the posture and expression of someone watching a horror movie, just sure that there was a jump scare coming up at any second. They all listened intently, the room in absolute silence.

After the routine introduction, Edwin's voice came in, low and uncertain. "Yeah, I...I don't know. I feel off. I've thought about it before, but maybe with a gun. But I know someone will have to clean it up, you know?" He laughed here, nervously, and added: "I was a Nirvana fan. When Kurt Cobain killed himself and those pictures from the scene were released years later...it chilled me. I thought it might be a good way to go out, but..."

"And why are you thinking of doing this, Edwin?"

Another nervous laugh, and then he answered with: "I wish I could explain it."

The borderline nonchalance in his voice had even Rachel feeling that he wasn't going to truly end his life. It was the same as dealing with problematic people pointing guns at other people. There were certain tones of voice and expressions that were indicators they would really never pull the trigger. She heard some of that in Edwin Newkirk's voice.

For the next nine minutes, they listened to Lisa expertly talk him down. By the end of the conversation, when Edwin's voice had leveled out and he told her that she'd been a huge help and he now had no intention of doing anything drastic, he sounded almost normal. The nervous undertones of his laughter were gone and he sounded truly grateful.

The final word of the call reminded Rachel of the way Joseph Staunton had sounded at the end of his call. Both men sounded almost embarrassed to have made the call in the first place. She could hear it clearly even in the simple "Bye" that ended the call.

Rachel and Jack exchanged a look, Jack giving a little nod. "Lisa, thank you for coming in to speak with us," Rachel said. "You can go now, unless Shelby has anything else?"

"No. Not at all. Great work, Lisa. I don't know that you could have handled those three any better."

Lisa stood up, wiping a tear away, and exited the room. Shelby turned her attention to the agents and shrugged. "Is that what you were looking for?"

"Yes," Jack said. "I think that proves that there was nothing suspicious about the calls. I suppose it really was just a coincidence." He sighed and got to his feet. "But all the same, thank you for your cooperation."

"Of course. And I certainly hope you can find out what's going on."

Rachel felt defeated as she and Jack were led out of the conference room and back out to the main lobby. She especially hated it when something that felt so solid turned out to be nothing more than a coincidence. Knowing that it happened more than people realized did not help her to accept it any easier.

Passing through the little lobby, she looked out the window, out to the streets of New York. Dusk wasn't here just yet, but it was fast approaching. And she had the strong inclination that a killer who had potentially hit three nights in a row would have no problem making it four in a row.

They needed to get to the precinct to mobilize as many officers as possible to make sure that didn't happen.

CHAPTER THIRTEEN

As night fell, Rachel and Jack made their first official visit to the precinct to meet with Detective Branson. FBI agents passing through a New York City precinct wasn't much of a big deal and Rachel was fully aware of this. However, when she and Jack piled into one of the station's conference rooms to come up with a game plan for the night, she felt that they were given the undivided attention of the dozen or so cops who had been assigned to assist with trying to prevent a fourth murder and maybe even find the killer.

There was a soft buzz circulating around the room as Rachel waited for Jack to end his conversation with the precinct chief. She saw them nod to one another and then shake hands before the chief rushed off elsewhere. Jack joined her at the front of the conference room and let Rachel have the floor. It was an uncontested fact between them that she was much better addressing a crowd of more than four or five than Jack was. He tended to get nervous and make unnecessary jokes, whereas Rachel was more to the point and direct. And while it had never really bothered Rachel to take the lead in situations like this, it was a bit different to look out and see numerous NYPD officers, all a bit on edge.

"Captain Yancy has, I'm sure, given you all the details, correct?" she asked.

A series of nods greeted her. All eyes were on her, as well as a few scanning the reports that had been placed on the table that sat between the agents and the twelve officers who had been assigned this particular duty.

"Three nights in a row, three potential victims, and three different bridges," Rachel said. "The only pattern we have is that if there is indeed a killer, they seem to be striking every night. I want to think that the difference in bridges might be relevant, too, but that would be a dangerous assumption to make.

"So what we've done is compiled a list of bridges that the most suicide attempts have been made from over the past decade. We'll need them monitored as much as possible tonight. Anything out of the ordinary—even as random as a lone pedestrian on a walk that stops for three seconds—needs to be checked out. Make sense?"

Again, she was met with mostly nods. A few of the officers looked irritated being given what was essentially a needle-in-a-haystack hunt.

"Yeah, but what if there's not even a murderer out there?" said a broad-shouldered officer in the back of the room. "You guys have said that it's just this third guy that seems like it might have been some sort of staged suicide. Are we really willing to put all of this manpower behind something like this if we don't even know for sure we're looking for a killer?"

"That's a good point," Jack said. "And if you want me to be honest, yeah, I'm struggling with that, too. But you can have a look at the reports yourself. A potential second person on the scene, likely a pusher, on the third jumper. Family members of two of the jumpers shocked that their loved ones would actually take their lives. It's worth looking into."

"And here's another thing," Rachel said. "If we were to find that there's a fourth jumper tomorrow morning, I think it takes any hope of it all being coincidental out of it. And I'd rather be safe than sorry." She regarded the room and could feel the stress of it all pressing in against her.

Without any warning at all, she felt herself growing dizzy. Her vision grew hazy for the briefest of moments. She did everything she could to lock her knees, to not even sway the slightest bit. *Right now?* she thought. *Really? Right now?* A faint pain stirred in her head like thunder and then faded away. The dizziness went away with it.

"And another thing," she said, trying to get her focus back. "The first victim was out in Cold Spring. So we don't even know if keeping the focus here in the city is going to be enough. We'll need to be ready to respond to any calls that might come from outside your jurisdiction as well. Thanks for your cooperation, everyone."

"Well, hold on," one of the officers said. "Where do you want us to start?"

"I have no problem admitting that I don't know this city well," Rachel said. "I'll leave it to you locals to figure out. If at any point you need assistance of any kind, Agent Rivers and I will be driving from checkpoint to checkpoint, so feel free to call."

The response was immediate. She'd never seen law enforcement respond so quickly. Officers were pairing off and instantly talking about the routes they'd take. The conference room was a flurry of activity and conversation with a game plan now in place. Now, the only thing left to do was get out on the field.

61

Rachel quickly found that driving between checkpoints was a task in and of itself. Driving around in one of the largest cities in the world and relying only on GPS made it difficult. She and Jack spent the first two hours of that night driving between numerous bridges, sometimes bypassing them and other times driving over them only to turn around and head back across in the opposite direction. She managed to make her way to Robert F. Kennedy Bridge, the Manhattan Bridge, Hells Gate Bridge, then over to Willis Avenue and Third Avenue Bridges. She stared to feel a little out of her depth, not having realized there were so many damned bridges in New York City.

Along the way, they got calls here and there about how different precincts from Queens and the Bronx were also pitching in where they could. But even then, it just felt like too much of a task.

On their way back from the Third Avenue Bridge, Rachel's phone made a noise that startled her at first, because it wasn't one she had ever heard much. Hearing it, though, she remembered that she'd set an alarm for 9:30 to remember to call Paige. It wasn't something she'd done in the past, but since one of her dreaded fears related to her diagnosis was not having enough time with her daughter, she'd decided to make it a priority.

"I'm going to pull over for a bit," she said as she killed the alarm. "Mommy time."

She found a parking spot between a coffee shop and a quaint little bakery. For most of her life, she'd always thought of New York as this magical place that she'd always be enamored with. This was her third time in the city; she'd come once as a child on a vacation with her parents that she could barely remember, and a second time early in her FBI career but she'd spent the entire time in a field office and hotel. Now she felt like the place was nothing but one big maze that had been intentionally set up to confuse her.

"I'm going to grab a coffee," Jack said, nodding to the coffee shop. "Feels like it's going to be a long night. You want anything?"

"A green tea would be great. Hot, please."

Jack gave her a thumbs-up and left her alone in the car. Rachel called Peter's phone right away via FaceTime and couldn't help but smile when Paige answered almost right away.

"Mommy!"

"Hey, kiddo. I see you're in your pajamas and ready for bed. Have you brushed your teeth?"

"Yep. And Daddy already read me a chapter out of my book."

"Good. So then you're all ready for bed when we get off of here. How was school today?"

"Oh, it was great! The book fair started today. And we had those really yummy chicken nuggets for lunch!" She then switched topics with that weird speed only young kids are capable of. "Daddy says you're in New York! That's where the Statue of Liberty is. And a bunch of museums."

"Yes, I know."

"Are you going to get to see the Statue of Liberty?"

"I don't think so, sweetie. This job is going to be a crazy one. I don't think I'll get much sightseeing time. But maybe we can all visit one day and see it together."

"Ooh, that would be so cool!"

Even though Paige's face lit up at the idea, the thought of her daughter in this city creeped her out. It was nothing against New York for sure, but the case. Rachel was starting to understand that this case was skewing her view of the city. It made her hate the traffic that much more, and made her frustration with the endless rows of streets even stronger.

"You won't be there for very long will you?" Paige asked.

"I just don't know, sweetie. It all depends on if—"

"Because with Great-Gramma Tate being sick and all, I didn't think you'd stay away for too long."

It took a second or two for Rachel to understand what had just happened. Somehow, Paige knew about Grandma Tate. Since she'd only told Peter and Jack, it was quite clear who she'd heard it from.

"Did Daddy tell you about that?"

"Yeah. But I don't think he meant to. He looked really sad after he told me. Mommy, is she going to be okay? Daddy said it might be something real bad."

Rachel swallowed down her fury at Peter long enough to wrap things up with Paige. And as she did, she felt that she was *far* too close to the very real moment that might eventually come when she had to answer these same questions about herself. It made her heart ache and she could feel tears forming in the corners of her eyes. It did not help that they were speaking through FaceTime and that she could see the confusion and hurt in her daughter's eyes.

"You know, that's a very big topic to talk about," Rachel said. "It's certainly not something we should talk about on the telephone. We'll make sure to talk about it as soon as I get home. Okay?"

"Yeah, okay," Paige said sadly.

"You go to sleep, okay? But can you put Daddy on before we hang up?"

"Yeah, he's right here. G'night, Mommy. I love you."

"I love you, too."

The phone was jostled a bit as Paige handed the phone over to Peter. She could tell that he was moving before he looked into the phone. She watched as the blurred screen moved from the soft darkness of Paige's room to the lights of the upstairs hallway. It shifted angles again and she saw Peter's face. He was frowning when he looked into the phone and said, "Rach, I'm so sorry."

"Jesus, Peter. That's probably something we should have told her together! Or better yet, to have waited until Grandma Tate came to visit."

"I know. It just sort of slipped out. I didn't even think of it until after it was out and…you know what? It's a lame excuse. But yeah, I'm sorry."

"She looked upset when she asked. How much did you tell her?"

"Not everything. I just told her that her great-grandmother was sick and that it seems to be serious. She doesn't know the eventual outcome yet." He sighed and said, "I can tell you're pissed. Do we just need to call it a night and not bother talking?"

She hated that the answer came so easily to her but it was out of her mouth before she could answer. "Yes, Peter. Yes, I think that's a good idea. Just try not to tell her anything else she doesn't need to know just yet."

"I know that, Rachel!"

She took a deep breath and tried to focus herself. Through the windshield, she saw Jack coming out of the coffee shop with their drinks. "Good night, Peter."

"Good night."

She ended the call instantly and tossed the phone into the console. She wanted to be furious with him and she supposed that was part of why she felt so betrayed. But she also knew that part of the reason she was so furious was because she once again felt herself balancing along that very thin line of Grandma Tate's situation mirroring her own. Dealing with Grandma Tate's diagnosis and having that conversation with Paige was going to be far too close to revealing her own truth. And the pain in Paige's eyes over the idea of her great-grandmother being very sick was only a precursor to what might lurk there if she knew her own mother was very sick, too.

Seeing that she was off of the phone, Jack got back into the car. He handed Rachel her tea and in a passive, casual manner, asked, "Everything good at home?"

"Yeah," she said, though she could taste resentment lurking in the anger she'd not yet been able to voice. "Everything is great."

She then started the car and took off in the direction of the next bridge on their list.

CHAPTER FOURTEEN

Dustin Adams parked in the corner lot of High Bridge Park and looked to the right. There, the High Bridge, the oldest bridge in New York City, loomed over the Harlem River. It was one of those sights Dustin had always heard about but never took the time to visit. He'd been living in New York City for almost eight years now and had somehow managed to never catch that bug most newcomers got. He'd never cared to visit the Statue of Liberty, or to stand dumbstruck at Christmas in Rockefeller Center. So he'd never cared much to come out to this old bridge that had been closed for a good amount of time, only to be reopened for bicyclists and pedestrians in the name of historic significance.

Now that he looked at it though, he had to admit that it did look sort of cool. The curvature and steel arches looked almost like something out of Gotham City from the *Batman* movies and comics. This only added to the tension and unease Dustin felt as he looked at it, though.

Truth be told, he wasn't quite sure why he was here. Well, he knew the *easy* answer to that question, but he knew there were deeper ramifications, too. He was here because the call he'd received on his cell phone an hour ago had told him to come. He didn't know why, and he wasn't sure who had even called. All he knew was that the few words the person on the other end had spoken had been enough to get him to go: *"Meet me at the very center of the High Bridge at two thirty or I'll send your wife those emails you've been hiding. If you see cops, you wait until they're gone and then go to the center of the bridge."*

Dustin had not had a chance to ask questions because the call ended after that. After leaving his house, he'd tried calling the number back, but no one had answered. He'd panicked a bit during the eighteen-minute drive between his apartment and High Bridge. The call had not woken his wife up, mainly because he kept his phone on vibrate after ten o'clock at night And even if he *did* leave his ringer on, he wasn't even sure it would wake her up. The woman slept like a rock. Still, he worried that she'd get up to use the bathroom or something and find him gone. And then what? What sort of excuse was he supposed to use then?

One problem at a time, he told himself as he got out of his car and hurried to the bridge. He knew it all looked a little suspect, or that he might be out *hoping* to get mugged or killed—a lonely, middle-aged man out for a stroll on an old bridge at 2:20 in the morning. But he'd do pretty much anything to ensure those emails never got to his wife.

He wasn't even sure how it had all happened. He'd been in a very low place last year. The depression had gotten to be too much, and he'd acted out of it. And though he was in a much better place now thanks to therapy and the right medicines, the secrets that rested in those emails were the one thing he was going to keep hidden come hell or high water.

Only...now someone knew about them. He had no idea how. During the drive to the bridge, he'd suspected it might be some sort of hacker. Or maybe someone from that dark period last year that he could not quite remember. There'd been a lot of drinking and a lot of excess, so he was sure there were at least a few blank spots in his memory. But for the life of him, he could not think of who might know about the emails and the information they contained.

Dustin closed in on the center of the old bridge. He could hear the sounds of the city just fine from here, like faraway birdcalls, but his footsteps seemed very loud on the pavement. He looked behind him, making sure there was no sudden police presence. The inclusion of staying away from cops in the instructions he'd been given did not make him feel better at all.

When he reached what he assumed to be the center of the bridge, Dustin stopped. He looked down to the dark waters of the Harlem River and found it peaceful. To think that about a year ago he had thought about jumping into this very same river (not from this bridge, but still...) was overwhelming. He really had come a long way. He thought of the emails and of how his life might change because of them. He knew it was selfish, but he didn't think it was fair that he had overcome addictions of several kinds and still had this possible life-altering bomb lurking out there.

Dustin checked his watch and saw that it was 2:32. It was only two minutes past the agreed upon time but it was enough to make him wonder if had has been some sort of prank. He feared that his wife would call at any moment, asking where the hell he was. Asking if he was with *her* again, if he'd gone back to his old ways. He looked back down to the water, churning almost silently in the darkness, and thought about the man he'd been a year ago, of all of the mistakes he'd willingly made and—

Something moved behind him. It was a quick thumping noise, like a footstep.

He turned to see who it was, not liking how fast it sounded.

Dustin wasn't even able to turn halfway around before he was slammed hard against the side of the bridge. This hurt bad enough, the wind rushing out of him and a pins and needles sensation rushing up his spine. But before he was even aware of these pains, he was acutely aware of someone lifting him by his legs, as if trying to trip him.

He had just enough time to get out "What are y—" before the world went upside down.

He banked his head on the side of the bridge and everything started swirling as he fell. *Falling,* he thought. *I'm falling. Who was up there? Who was it and how did they know—*

That final thought was never fully formed as he slammed into the dark, waiting water and the life rushed right out of him.

CHAPTER FIFTEEN

At 2:10 a.m., Rachel and Jack were prepared to call it a night and head out to find a hotel. There had been zero reports and due to the late hour, a few pairs of officers were able to set up stakeout situations around some of the more prominent bridges on the list. As they made the decision to call it a night, Rachel's phone rang. The display showed a New York City area code and she felt a bit of hope stirring within her. Maybe this would be a cop. Maybe they finally had some sort of a break.

"This is Agent Gift," she answered.

"Well, damn," said a man with a thick northern accent. "Sorry, Agent. This is Officer Wachowski. Thought we had something for you that came over the radio. A seventeen-year-old kid loitering on the side of the Pulaski Bridge. Turns out he was dealing pot. But I literally just got that update when the phone started ringing."

"No worries, Officer. Thanks for being so prompt, if nothing else." She looked to Jack in the passenger seat and said, "False alarm."

He nodded as they both settled into the same forlorn understanding. They'd given instructions to call them right away if anything was found, if anything even *resembled* a suicide attempt from the side of a bridge. At the same time, they'd been going for nearly twenty hours now (well, Rachel had; she didn't know when Jack had woken up the previous night) and they both needed to get at least a few hours of sleep under their belt.

"Are you tired, Jack?"

"Eh, I'm okay. If you're feeling guilty about the notion of getting to sleep, I feel the same, though. I'm good to pull a few more hours if you are."

"Yeah, I think I'm good for that. I'm going to need you to drive for a bit. The GPS voice and all these streets and bridges…I feel like I'm in one of those escape rooms, you know?"

"No worries there. I'll drive for a few hours."

They swapped seats and Jack headed out toward the Williamsburg Bridge. They both doubted that the killer (if there *was* a killer) would revisit the same scene, but it was just a few streets away and none of the officers on patrol had rolled by there in over half an hour.

Sitting in the passenger seat and watching the dark, yet somehow also illuminated New York City streets pass by was both peaceful and anxiety-inducing all at once. She found herself revisiting that scary moment on the Williamsburg Bridge earlier in the day, wondering what it might be like to jump. To feel the wind, the loss of stability, the freedom.

If she'd been asked a month ago if anything could happen in her life that would cause her to commit suicide, she would have said no. But now here she was, finding a way to romanticize it. The anger she still felt toward Peter for dropping the news about Grandma Tate to Paige still sat heavy on her. It hurt to admit it to herself, but she thought if there was no Paige, she might very well start considering suicide as a way out of this mess. She thought she might take a cue from Grandma Tate and do her best to live another few good months, but as the end came she would want to go out on her own terms. And honestly, jumping seemed like a halfway decent way to go.

"None of this lines up with the other staged suicide cases we worked on, you know?" Jack's voice tore her out of her suicidal musings and she had to backtrack her mind just to understand what he'd said.

"Well, with those two cases, it was people who *clearly* would have never killed themselves. The suicide notes were awful and did not line up with handwriting or even word usage, according to the family members. In those cases, the so-called suicides came out of nowhere. With these three, there's at least a history of depression and vocal discussions with someone about their desire to end their own lives."

"So it's not random like the others," Rachel said. "I've thought about that and you know…you having just said it, I think the most important part of these three are that they were also seeking help. Finding three suicidal people is one thing. But finding three people that all wanted to find help to get rid of those thoughts is yet another."

"Unless it's just a spooky coincidence like all three of them calling the same hotline and ending up speaking to the same operator."

"So then what else could they have been looking into?" she wondered out loud. "We could look into doctors, pharmacies where they got their meds, or we—"

Her phone rang, startling her. Before picking it up from the console, she looked to the display and again saw a New York area code. She answered it quickly, daring to hope there might be promising news on the other end—yet also morbidly aware that promising news might end up resulting in someone's death.

70

"This is Agent Gift."

"Agent Gift, this is Officer Gretchen Carlisle. I'm currently rushing to High Bridge in Harlem. We've got reports of a body hitting the water in the Harlem Bridge."

Rachel covered the mouthpiece and told Jack. Then, returning her attention to the call, she asked: "How long ago?"

"The call came in less than five minutes ago from a cop in the area, checking over parking spots for tickets. We can't yet confirm that it's a body, but the cop on the scene said he's quite sure he also heard a brief shout or scream of some kind before the splash."

"Thank you, Officer Carlisle. We'll meet you there as soon as possible. Can you make a call to have officers stationed at both ends of the bridge until we get there?"

"Already done it."

Rachel ended the call and typed *High Bridge* into her GPS. Her heart surged with dread and adrenaline as the robotic voice told them where to go. Another body. Another person dead. And if she was being honest with herself, she was starting to feel absolutely bone-tired.

Even worse, they still had no leads…just a robotic voice directing them around a city she was wholly unfamiliar with. It was a different experience to hear that voice and not be the one driving, but she was thankful for it. She stared ahead into the night, any thoughts of getting some rest now far from her mind, as Jack followed the GPS into Harlem.

***

There was very clearly a body floating face down in the Harlem River. Rachel could see it from the mouth of the bridge as nothing more than a speck of white and dark blue clothing, and a muddled mess of wet hair. The body was bobbing lazily, not yet carried any real distance from the bridge. She and Jack raced up over the bridge to where several members of the NYPD were already huddled together. Flashlight beams hovered in the darkness, illuminating faces and feet alike. A few officers were looking down with great interest from where it appeared the man had jumped from.

"Anything of note yet?" Rachel asked.

"Well," one of the cops said, "it's a tough call because it's night, but there appears to be just the slightest amount of blood right here along the side of the bridge." He aimed his flashlight over the side and pointed it out. Sure enough, there was a fresh smear of blood along the steel side. He had been right in that it wasn't much at all. Maybe just enough to come from a head that accidentally struck the side on the way down.

Rachel considered this for a moment and then looked to Jack. "If someone is jumping off a bridge, they'd get decent distance, right? At least a few feet? No way in hell they're going to hit their head on the side. Now, if they were pushed..."

She left the thought unfounded as Jack thought it over. "No one was found on the scene after the initial call?"

"There were two people that were originally suspects. One was a waitress heading home from her shift at a Waffle House. We already called the supervisor to confirm it and she checked out. The other was a guy out doing some sort of New York at Night vlog or some nonsense. I think they're still questioning him on the other side of the bridge, but the footage he shot has him five blocks away from here when the traffic cop made the original call."

"The body looks way too far out to get to," Jack said. "How deep does this river get?"

"It depends on the time of year but right now it's probably about ten or twelve feet beneath where we're standing."

"They're on the way up the river with a patrol boat right now," said another officer. This one was female, and Rachel noted the name above her left breast read Carlisle. "Detective Branson is on his way as well."

"Thanks. And nice to have a face to go with the name. Officer Carlisle, I wonder if I could borrow your flashlight?"

Carlisle handed it over without question. Rachel used it to look around the bridge, looking for anything at all that might serve as some sort of indicator of what had happened. If it was a case of a simple jump, there'd be nothing. But if there *was* some sign of a second party, she intended to find it. The walking space consisted of stable wooden planks

As she searched, she became aware of someone approaching her. She thought it was Jack at first, but it turned out to be Detective Branson. "Sorry it took so long," he said. "It's been a crazy night with everyone stretched thin because of this. I've also been talking with the Department of Parks and Recreation to get our hands on the CCTV footage from the cameras over at Highbridge Park. It's a long shot, but worth checking, I'd think."

"For sure."

"Are you looking for anything in particular?"

"I don't know. I'm just thinking that if there was someone who pushed our victim, there's nowhere to really sneak up on them from. They had to have been lying in wait, maybe even down on the ground. But I can't see anything that points to that."

Someone else came hurrying over and this time it *was* Jack. "The boat just showed up," he said, hitching a thumb over his shoulder. Rachel looked in that direction and saw a small floodlight beaming out, scanning the water and falling just shy of the floating body.

As Rachel and Jack walked back down the way they'd come, to the Manhattan side of the bridge, a few of the other officers started to head out and go their separate ways. Four others, including Carlisle and Branson, hung around to see the scene out.

They watched from the foot of the bridge as the patrol boat drew closer to the body. It was carefully hauled on board and there was very little pause between securing the body and puttering over to land. As it neared land, the driver killed the engine and it coasted over to them until it softly banged against the bank just off the base off the archway on the Manhattan side.

Aside from the driver and the officer in the boat with him, Rachel and Jack were the first to see the body. The man was male, likely in his early forties. He had light brown hair made dark by the water, and his wide open eyes were also brown. Right away, Rachel saw the nasty abrasion on the right side of his head. It looked almost like road rash, the blood still flowing, albeit not quite as much as the stain on the side of the bridge would have led her to believe. Then again, if he'd been face down in the water, the blood flow had likely slowed considerably.

Other than the scrape on the side of his head, there were no clear signs of injury. She knew that most suicides into water often broke their pelvis and several ribs but none of that would be verifiable until he was placed on an examination table.

"Anyone got evidence gloves?" she asked.

Branson, who'd appeared as if from nowhere, handed her a pair from the inner pocket of his suit coat. She slipped them on and pressed solidly against the man's right side in a few places. She was pretty sure she felt at least two broken ribs.

"Thoughts?" the boat driver said.

"Plenty. But the most jarring one is that this is four bodies in four nights, all apparent suicides. And I think it now goes far beyond coincidence."

CHAPTER SIXTEEN

Because the body was in such good condition, just about every possible avenue for identification was available to them. Rachel, fighting off exhaustion with a cup of precinct coffee that tasted just a few grades above diesel fuel, was sitting in a small conference room with Jack when Branson came into the room. He tossed a thin folder down onto the table and collapsed into one of the available chairs. Apparently, he'd not slept for quite some time, either.

"The victim is thirty-nine-year-old Dustin Adams. He worked as an insurance claims adjuster and lived in Brooklyn. As we speak, there's a unit headed over to his residence to inform his wife. I figure if you guys want to act fast, I can head over there and talk to her, too. Maybe give it about half an hour or so."

"I appreciate it," Rachel said, "but I'd like to speak with her. And I'd like to do it sooner rather than later. If he wasn't the type to consider suicide, I want to hear a genuine, raw reaction from her. Because honestly, if he was the sort to do it, I think we're more likely to hear it when the wound is still fresh."

She realized just how morbid that sounded, but it was the truth. She downed the rest of her coffee and asked, "Can you text me the address?"

"Yeah," Branson said.

"And I need his phone records. Can you get someone on that, too?"

"Of course. Branson sounded both tired and a little impressed at the same time. As he started typing the address into a text message, Rachel and Jack headed back out to their rental car less than two hours after Dustin Adams had been pulled out of the Harlem River.

Following the GPS once again based on the address Brandon had given them, they had to take a course that, for just a moment, offered a view of the archway of the High Bridge. In an odd way, it almost felt as if they were being haunted.

"So with the phone records," Jack said as they close in on Dustin Adams's address. "Just what the hell are we supposed to do if Better Days pops up again? If we're saying four murders can no longer be ruled a coincidence, I don't think that could, either."

"I don't know. I think we'll have to figure that one out when there's nowhere else to look."

When they arrived at the apartment building, there was already a patrol car parked out front. Rachel felt guilty for the relief she felt. It was hard enough talking to a woman who was learning that she'd recently been made a widow, but delivering news of the suicide was an entirely different sort of torture.

Dustin Adams had lived on the second floor, in Apartment 28. As Rachel and Jack approached the door, they could already hear wailing. Undeterred, Rachel knocked softly on the door. It was answered almost at once by a haggard-looking officer. He was young, but had a lumberjack beard that made him look more rugged than he likely was.

Jack showed his ID first, making introductions. "Agents Rivers and Gift."

The bearded officer nodded. "We were told you'd be coming. The wife is in shock, but she can still talk. I don't think she's accepted it just yet."

"Any kids?" Jack asked.

"No."

Rachel found relief in that, as adding children—even ones that were adults and moved away—made situations like this infinitely sadder. The bearded officer led them through the small hallway that emptied out into a living room and adjoining kitchen. A woman sat with a second officer on a couch against the back wall. The officer looked very uncomfortable and maybe even out of his element. The woman, meanwhile, looked up as Rachel, Jack, and the bearded officer came into the room. There was a dazed look on her face and though it was clear she'd done a good deal of wailing and crying, there was a confused aspect to her expression. It was almost as if, though heartbroken, she was expecting someone to jump from behind a corner somewhere and tell her this was all part of a cruel prank.

The bearded officer took up a space at the intersection of the living room and kitchen. "Mrs. Adams, these are Agents Rivers and Gift. Is it okay if they ask you a few questions?"

Mrs. Adams nodded, slowly turning her eyes to the agents. "This is all a mistake," she said. "It has to be a mistake. Dustin...he wouldn't do this. There's no way he...no way..."

"That's why we'd like to talk to you," Rachel said, coming forward and making sure to keep her voice soft and reassuring. "I need to be blunt here for a moment, so please forgive me. But your husband will be the fourth person that appears to have taken his own life in the last

75

four days. However, there are some signs that indicate they may not have been suicides at all. Right now, the sheer number of instances is essentially a clue in and of itself. You seem confident that your husband would not take his own life. And if you can, I need you to tell me why."

The wife nodded and made a strange gulping noise that Rachel assumed was her desperate attempt to keep some sort of control, to keep a flood of grief from pouring out of her.

"Dustin had spent some time working through a variety of issues. He had a rough childhood—some pretty traumatic things with his parents that were always difficult for him to talk about. It led to bouts with depression and yes, a few years back, he locked himself in the bathroom with a razor. But he's worked so hard...he's come out of all of that and..."

Sensing the woman on the brink of losing it, Rachel did her best to press on. She knew their time here was limited and that the woman needed to properly grieve. The last thing Rachel wanted was to get in the way of that.

"Was he seeing a therapist at any point?"

"Yes. He still sees one. The same therapist that helped him back then. But even she said he had vastly improved—that the current appointments were mostly just continual check-ups."

"What about meds?"

"Yes, he took a few different medicines over the years. But those had been cut back, too, as he improved. The only one he still takes is Paxil."

Rachel noted that Mrs. Adams was still referring to her husband in the present tense. It was jarring because she knew that in about a year's time, her own family would have to deal with this sort of thing—thinking of her as a thing gone, a thing of the past that was no longer with them.

"When was the last time you thought he might be slightly depressed?" Rachel asked. "Even if it was a small moment here or there?"

"That's just it," she said, tears coming down the sides of her face as her voice took on a fragile little waver. "He was happy. He'd been happy for the better part of a year. I just...I thought it was all behind him. No...I *know* it was all behind him. This isn't right. This can't be happening." Slowly, she started to lose control of herself then. She began to tremble and shake, looking to the four people in her living room with wide, pleading eyes. "It's not really Dustin, is it? Are you sure? I mean...no, it can't be, right? *Right?*"

A knock at the door interrupted her. Again the bearded man hurried to it. When he answered it, there were no introductions. All Rachel heard was a rushed "I'm her sister" as a younger woman came rushing into the apartment. She so closely resembled Mrs. Adams that Rachel thought the two women might actually be twins. When Mrs. Adams saw her sister, she sprang from the couch and the women met in the center of the room.

Mrs. Adams wailed into her sister's shoulder. Rachel could actually feel the shrieking in her bones. She turned her head away from it and nodded to Jack, tilting her head and gesturing for him to join her out in the hallway.

They closed the door behind them, but the screams and cries of the newly widowed Mrs. Adams could still be heard clearly.

"He saw a therapist," Rachel said. "He was taking meds, he *used to be* in a bad place and struggled with depression, and then he seemed better. And now he's supposed to have jumped to his death. It feels far too much like the others."

"Yeah, I'd say so, too. I think it's safe to say we're definitely dealing with a killer here. But we're still running blind. No leads, no clues, no witnesses."

"Maybe there will be something in his phone records. And maybe if we light a fire under the bureau's ass, they'll get us results on those incoming private numbers." All of this was true, but what she was really rushing toward was a much simpler request: if there was no real reason for them to be here around this agony and loss, she wanted to leave. Because even though she felt she'd managed to distance herself from it all and to draw a very distinct line between her diagnosis and the duties of her job, being around a woman who had just lost her spouse was feeling a little too close to home.

"Let's go find out, then," he said. "Hold on a second, and I'll tell the officers to fill us in if anything pops up—and for Mrs. Adams to call us if she thinks of anything that might be at all relevant."

He went back inside to do this and when he opened the door, the screams had become high-pitched whines as Mrs. Adams tried to draw in breaths between her sobs and shrieks. *That's going to be Peter in about a year,* some deep-seated voice inside of her said. *If you'd let him know what's going on, he'll at least be prepared.*

As if to put an exclamation point on this thought, Mrs. Adams let out another scream, this one taking the form of her dead husband's

77

name. It pierced some part of Rachel's heart that she'd managed to keep mostly hidden since receiving the diagnosis. Feeling a sense of pain and guilt that had so far remained mostly distant, Rachel did not wait for Jack. She turned away from the apartment door and headed to the car, as if trying to outrun the wails of that poor widow.

CHAPTER SEVENTEEN

When Rachel and Jack arrived back at the precinct twenty minutes later, a frazzled-looking officer rushed up to them as soon as they made their way back to the conference room they had claimed as the temporary hub of operations for the case. He had a thin stack of papers in his hands, which he waved at them as he approached.

"Detective Branson told me to give these to you as soon as I had them," the officer said, thrusting the papers at Rachel.

She took them and saw that the five pages, still warm from the printer, were Dustin Adams's phone records, dating back four months. She was a bit shocked that they'd gotten them so fast but then again, this fourth victim had upped the severity of an already tragic case. She hoped they could expect this sort of speed and efficiency from here on out.

Rachel scanned the pages as she and Jack made their way into the conference room. She had not even sat down before she found the two things she was specifically looking for. First and foremost, there was yet another call from a private number. In Dustin's case, it had come the day before his death. What she did not see at first was a call to Better Days Prevention Hotline in the days leading up to it. Yet as she looked through the records, she did see the number pop up from three weeks in the past.

"Okay, so we divide and conquer," Jack said. "You call Shelby at Better Days and see if Lisa took this call three weeks ago when Dustin called. If she did…I don't even know. I know she's probably free of anything related to this case, but that's just too much to look beyond."

"And you?"

"I'll get on the phone with the bureau to light a fire under someone to get me the information on these private numbers. If I have to, I'll shake it up the tree straight to Director Anderson."

With a game plan in mind, they went to separate sides of the room. As she pulled up the number Shelby had given her while visiting Better Days, Rachel found that she truly hoped it would turn out that Lisa had not spoken with Dustin Adams. She was all but certain Lisa had nothing to do with the crimes—that she was simply the recipient of an insane amount of bad luck and coincidence. To put her through yet another session of what she'd experienced this morning almost seemed like torture.

The phone rang and Shelby answered right away. "Better Days Prevention Hotline, this is Shelby."

"Shelby, it's Agent Gift again. I hate to say it, but there's been another one. A fourth victim that appears to have been a jumper but…well, there's enough at the scene to make us think it may have been foul play." Even as she said this, she could see that streak of fresh blood on the side of the bridge.

"My God. Agent Gift…this is unprecedented. Are you now certain they're murders?"

"I'm becoming more and more certain of it, yes. But there's another thing. We've just received phone records for the fourth victim. It's a man by the name of Dustin Adams. He called your hotline three weeks ago. I know it's a very long shot, but we have to be sure…"

"You want to know if he spoke with Lisa."

"Yes. Could you find that out, please?"

"Of course," Shelby said. Her voice was thin and sad, as if she were deathly afraid of what they were on the cusp of discovering. "I just need the phone number and the time he called in."

Rachel read her the information off of the records. She listened to the light clattering of fingers on keys for a moment as Jack started speaking into his phone on the other side of the room. Several seconds later, when Shelby started speaking again, Rachel already knew what the answer was going to be; she could hear the relief in the woman's voice.

"Lisa did not take a call from that number. That call was taken by one of our more senior volunteers. Do you think you'll need to speak with her as well?"

"Right now, I'm honestly not too sure. Maybe sometime later down the road. Thank you for your help to this point."

"Sure. I'm glad to help in any way I can."

They ended the call and Rachel made her way over to where Jack was standing, speaking into his phone. She sat at the edge of the table and listened in. She also grabbed a marker from the conference room table and jotted a message down on the back of the last page of Dustin Adams's phone records: IT WASN'T LISA. She showed it to him and he gave her a thumbs-up as he continued with his call.

"Okay," he was saying, "and how long will that take? Yeah? Jesus, fine. Okay. Yes, I'll take what you have. I need it like yesterday."

He ended his call and though he sounded flustered, it did not reflect on his face. "Okay, so naturally, they won't have this new one for a while. And they're having trouble cracking the private number that came through to Nick Harding. But we do have positive IDs on the private numbers that came through to Joseph Staunton and Edwin Newkirk. They're sending that over right now."

Even as he finished saying this, he was scrolling through his emails. He nodded and Rachel watched as he tapped on an email that had just come in. He read it over, his brow cinching up a bit and making it hard to read his expression.

"Well?" Rachel asked.

"The first number is to a psychiatrist in Brooklyn. That's the private number off of Joseph Staunton's records. I suppose that makes sense, if he had been seeing a psychiatrist. A simple phone call can clear that one up. But this second one...the one from Newkirk's records is from a cell phone here in the city. But it's somehow unlisted. Makes me think it may have come from a dummy phone. Maybe one of those burner deals."

"But those can still be tracked, right?" Rachel said.

"Right," Jack said, already dialing up the bureau again. After a few seconds, he spoke urgently into the phone. "Yeah, me again. I need you to ping that cell phone. Yeah, it's unlisted, but if it's a dummy phone, it can still be traced, right?" There was a brief pause as the person on the other end responded and then Jack ended with: "Call me when you get a hit."

He ended the call and they looked at one another. It was an odd moment for any case—to feel such a sense of possible momentum but having to wait for someone else to deliver the information needed to get moving again.

"You think the psychiatrist Staunton was seeing will be any help?" Jack asked.

"Doubtful. Because he's already passed, I doubt they're going to see fit to breach doctor-patient confidentiality. If he was still alive and we had it on good authority that he planned to hurt someone...maybe."

"Also," Rachel said, "even though Lisa has been ruled out as the operator that spoke to Dustin Adams on the hotline, I can't quite let that go. I mean, all four of our victims called the same hotline. I mean, even if the operators and Shelby weren't under scrutiny, I think the case could be argued that they may not be very good at what they do."

"I thought the same thing," Jack said. "But we both heard the recordings of those calls. If Lisa's skillset is any indicator, I'd say

81

they're all pretty good at their jobs. And that then leads me to think the hotline has nothing to do with it. I do have to acknowledge the coincidental nature of it all, though."

While they waited for Jack's contact to call back, they looked over the phone records one more time, looking for any other similarities. But all they found was that three of the four had eaten pizza from the same chain over the past three weeks, though from different locations.

It seemed like it took forever for Jack's call to come, but Rachel's own phone told her it had only been nine minutes. When Jack answered the call, he placed it on speaker mode so Rachel could hear as well.

"I like the speed you guys have going over there," Jack joked. "You got a name and location for me?"

"I've got an address," a deep yet chipper male voice responded. "It's a cell phone, so if the user was moving, we'd see that. But this user is stationary and, from what I can see, is actively using the phone right now. I didn't get a name, like I said, which makes me think it's either an illegal burner-type phone or one of those pay-as-you-go deals."

"Got an address?"

The man on the other line did have an address, and he recited it slowly. Rachel jotted down on the same sheet of the report she'd penned his message concerning Lisa's innocence. Jack gave a quick "Thank you" and ended the call.

Rachel got to her feet, slapping at the address on the paper. "Okay. Looks like we're heading back to Brooklyn."

"Figures," Jack said. "I'd really love to wrap this thing and not have to cross another damned bridge."

Rachel knew he meant it as a joke, but there was nothing at all funny about the uneasy tone in his voice.

CHAPTER EIGHTEEN

Rachel's limited knowledge of the city once again showed itself when she was surprised to find that the Brooklyn address was leading them right back to the Williamsburg area—the same area where Edwin Newkirk had allegedly jumped from the Williamsburg Bridge to end his life. She was starting to get used to the congested traffic and the often maze-like structure of the streets but she still felt anxious and almost discouraged when they finally made it to the address.

It was another typical apartment building, the dingy and generic sort Rachel had seen in countless TV shows and movies featuring New York City: five or six stories with a fire escape along the side, bordered by similar buildings on both sides. Before they got out of the car, Jack pulled up the number of his contact back in DC. If they knocked on the door and their suspect wasn't home any longer, they may have to rely on the guy in DC to help them track the now-moving phone.

When they got out of the car and walked to the front of the building, Rachel noted that the streets were fairly busy. Pedestrians hurried along on the sidewalks, and traffic remained steady on the road. It *was* nearing noon, though, so she assumed some of this crowd could be the result of people trying to get a jumpstart on lunch breaks.

After climbing the concrete stairs to the front of the building, they discovered that there was no lock on the building's front doors, allowing them to go right inside. The address they'd been given stated that the man they did not yet have a name for lived in Apartment 401. They took the elevator up, the small metal box scarred and marked up by countless years of abuse. Rachel could feel her muscles tensing, her instincts telling her that they could very well be less than one minute away from their first substantial break in this case.

The elevator stopped and they stepped out into the hallway. The elevator had placed them in the center of the hall, so they walked to the right, toward Apartment 401. They approached as casually as possible and when they came to the door, Jack knocked without so much as a single pause. There was no response of any kind. Rachel leaned closer, her ear less than three inches from the door as she knocked this time. Again, there was nothing from the other side.

"You sure this is the right place?" she asked.

"This is the address I was given. I suppose he could have left. It's been about half an hour since we got the address."

"Call your guy and see if he can figure it out."

Jack did as she asked while they walked back to the elevator. As he spoke to his contact, Rachel kept her eye on the door to Apartment 401 but it was never answered. It did seem a little strange that according to Jack's bureau contact, the phone's owner had been there half an hour ago and now, with the FBI coming to knock on his door, he was gone. She tried not to read too much into it, though, as Jack quickly updated the man on the other end of the phone.

"He's not here anymore," Jack said. "Now that you've already tapped into the phone, how hard is it for you to get it back up?"

Rachel hated only hearing one side of the conversation, but she also understood Jack's reasoning for not putting it on speaker. If there *was* someone in Apartment 401, standing by the door and listening to what might be going on outside in the hallway moments after she and Jack had knocked, a call on speaker mode would only heighten suspicion.

"Okay, yeah, that's great," Jack said. "Yes, we're in the apartment building right now." After a few more seconds, Jack pushed the Down button on the elevator console. The doors opened right away. "Getting on the elevator. Give me a second, would you?"

Jack stepped into the elevator, Rachel following behind. "What's he saying?" Rachel asked.

"He says the phone's owner has moved, but he's close by. No more than two blocks from what he can tell. But he's also saying that he can only get about a block or so accurate if the owner is not inside a building."

They took the elevator down and hurried outside. When they were back on the street, Jack got back on the phone. "Okay. We're out. Which direction?"

The man gave an answer and Jack motioned Rachel to follow him. He headed to the right, in the direction of a hot dog vendor and a busy intersection. As they walked quickly that way, Rachel was again shocked by the number of people that were filling the streets. If they could only get within a block's accuracy, this was going to be a lot harder than they'd thought.

As she scanned the people on the streets, she also did her best to stay tuned in to Jack's conversation. "How much farther?" Then, after about twenty seconds of the other man speaking, Jack said, "Are you kidding me? How in the hell are we supposed to...yeah, okay. Yeah, that's a good idea."

With that, he ended the call and though he continued to walk forward, it was clear that he did so with no clear direction.

"What did he say?" Rachel asked.

"That we're within a block of the guy. It could be any one of these people on the street."

"Do we know for sure he'd be out here?"

"It's almost certain. He *could* be in a building, but it seems that he's still on the move. We missed him at his apartment by mere minutes."

They came to the hot dog vendor, just shy of the intersection. She guessed there might be twenty-five or thirty people on the streets within the block up ahead. A few were actively speaking on their phones while a handful of others were walking along while also looking at something on their phones.

"Do you have the number?" she asked as an idea occurred to her.

"Yeah. Why?"

"Call it. And if someone answers, ask for Bob. Then apologize that you called the wrong number."

"Genius," he said, pulling the number up. She watched as he made the call and then looked out to the crowd from their place behind the hot dog vendor.

She was standing close enough to Jack that she could just barely hear the ringing of the other line. She scanned the crowd, looking for someone who was taking the time to stop to answer a call. She saw nothing like this, though she heard Jack start to speak.

"Hey! Is this Bob?" A pause, and then Jack putting on a great performance. "Ah hell, sorry about that. Must be a wrong number."

Just as he ended the call, Rachel saw a man half a block away, standing on the opposite side of the street in front of a thrift store. He was removing his phone from his ear and held it in front of him. He was looking at the screen with a confused expression and then placed it back into his pants pocket.

"I think I got him," Rachel said. "Wait a few seconds and call him again."

She kept her eyes on the suspect as he started walking across the street. He looked to be studying the road and the cars that came and went. It made her wonder if he might be looking to hail a cab. As he passed across the street, she almost lost him as he walked behind three others that were also crossing the street. She saw him clearly as he came to the sidewalk, though. He started walking away from them, his back to them.

"Come on," Rachel said. They left their spot behind the hot dog vendor and carefully made their way across the street. Rachel could still see the man, about half a block away. He seemed to be in no real hurry.

"Okay, call it again," she said. "If he answers, don't say a word."

Jack placed the call again. Within two seconds, the man Rachel had been spying on stopped walking and reached back into his pocket. He pulled out his phone, checked the caller display, and pressed a button on the side. He then returned it to his pocket.

"Voicemail," Jack said.

"Then there's our guy," she said, nodding ahead.

Rachel took the lead and broke into a hurried walk. She knew that breaking into a run in a crowded street would do nothing but alert their man and give him reason to run away. As they advanced, the man became a bit clearer. He was of average build and height and was wearing a pair of jeans and a blue T-shirt with a brand logo on the front. She guessed him to be in his late thirties or early forties. He was also wearing a cap that covered his hair, making an accurate estimation difficult.

While they continued to close the gap between them, the suspect seemed to still be looking for a cab. In doing so, he spotted Rachel and Jack. Rachel tried to halt her progress—to appear as if she was not in a big hurry to get to him—but he'd seen her too quickly. She had just enough time to see a worried look cross his face before he took off. He ran back across the street, instantly drawing the ire of two drivers who blared their horns at him.

"Shit!" Rachel turned hard to the left, watching for traffic as she bounded out into the street. She held a hand out to ward off oncoming traffic, knowing it likely meant next to nothing in New York City. Still, she managed to get across the street safely, with Jack coming in behind her and blaring horns escorting them along.

The entire time, Rachel never took her eyes off of the suspect. He was fast, but his panic was causing him to run carelessly. He was bumping into pedestrians and kept looking back at them, slowing his progress. When he came to the end of the block, he turned left and continued down the sidewalk. When Rachel rounded that same corner, she saw that the sidewalk was a bit more open here. There was far less foot traffic, which allowed for the suspect to run faster.

But it also meant that Rachel could run faster as well. She kicked in an extra bit of speed, and at the same moment her body truly felt in tune and at its maximum performance, she recalled what had happened the last time she chased a suspect with this same kind of power. She'd been in pursuit of a protestor outside of a fertility clinic, just a few days after getting her terrible diagnosis from her doctor. During the chase, she'd blacked out and spent the rest of the case dodging question from Jack.

"Sir, you need to stop," she yelled. "We're with the FBI! You run, it looks worse for you!"

The comment put just enough hesitation in the man's step to make the chase much less competitive. As Rachel closed in on him, Jack caught up to her. Side by side, they closed in on the man and this time Jack gave it a try.

"We're FBI agents! Sir, you need to stop right now!"

Up ahead, the end of the block came into view. It was blocked off from the next block by a steady stream of traffic. The suspect tried coming to a hard halt in order to turn left again, but doing so caused him to lose his footing. He gained his balance before hitting the ground but the misstep allowed Rachel and Jack to catch him before he could start down another street.

Jack bore down on him, and Rachel fell in behind the suspect. They had him cornered and they both had their hands positioned over their holstered Glocks.

"What's your name, sir?" Rachel asked between gasps for breath. She hadn't felt just how much the sprinting had taken out of her until she started speaking.

The man looked up at them with wild, bewildered eyes. "You're running me down in the street and don't even know my fucking name? What's wrong with you?"

"Your unlisted phone number has been present on the phone records of a number of recently murdered men," Jack said. "We'd like to know why."

"Murdered men? What are you even talking about?"

"We'll explain everything in a moment," Rachel said. "For now, you're going to need to come with us."

"And if I don't?"

"A formal arrest for running away from a federal agent. Your choice."

The man thought it over for a moment, looking back and forth between the agents. With defeat and, Rachel thought, a bit of fear in his voice, he said, "Fine. I'll talk."

"Good," Rachel said. "Again, what is your name?"

"Alberto Spears," he said. He didn't so much say this as spit it out.

"And what do you—"

"Oh, I think there's been a misunderstanding," Spears interrupted. "You have my name, and that's it. I'll talk...but not until I've contacted my lawyer."

"Have it your way," Jack said, reaching for his cuffs. "But usually people don't ask to speak to a lawyer until they're officially under arrest."

Spears looked at Jack almost teasingly and offered his forearms. "Then here you go."

Jack didn't hesitate to slap the cuffs around his wrists. They escorted Alberto Spears to their car with Rachel feeling at odds with just how easy this all suddenly seemed.

CHAPTER NINETEEN

Spears didn't talk for very long. In fact, once he was in the back seat of the car, he clammed up. In the silence, Rachel noticed Jack sending a text on his cell phone. She saw that it was going to Detective Branson and, at a stoplight, saw what he was sending. He was requesting that a unit be sent to Alberto Spears's address to see if anything of importance could be found in relation to the four victims. Not aware of this, Alberto sat in the back and maintained his silence all the way to the precinct, and even during his escorted walk to an interrogation room.

Rachel accompanied him into the room first, followed by Jack. As Jack was about to close the door, someone else rushed to stop him. It was Detective Branson, stopping in the doorway with an excited look on his face.

"Promising?" he asked them quietly.

"Could be," Jack said.

"The thing is," Rachel added, "he's making us wait until his lawyer gets here before he'll give us anything. But he *has* given us a name. Alberto Spears. Think you could run a background check for us?"

"Sure," Branson said. It was clear he knew the approach Rachel was taking. It was a process of applying intimidation without actually making any direct threats. "You got an address?"

"Yeah," Jack said. He gave him the address his contact in DC had provided them with. He then turned back to Alberto, sitting at the table in the center of the room. The man looked a little spooked now, the direct and stubborn façade he'd put on in the back of the car crumbling very fast. "You sure you don't want to at least give us the bare details before I send this New York City detective to get your information? It's going to look much better on you in the end if you offer it willingly."

"I don't even know what the hell you want, man!"

"We have four bodies on our hands," Rachel said. "And when we pulled their phone records, your unlisted number was on them." This was stretching the truth a bit, she knew. It was only confirmed that the number had been on two of the records; she was hoping he might trip himself up and admit to more than they already had.

"I don't know anything about that."

"The deaths looked like suicides," Rachel said. "Does that help?"

Alberto said nothing, but he went pale. Behind them, perhaps sensing that the agents had the situation covered, Branson started to close the door. Before he left, though, he added: "Just let me know if you need that background check run. I can have it in ten minutes."

"Thanks, Detective," Jack said. "Oh, and that other thing I texted you about earlier. Where are we with that?"

"Oh, it's going down right now. We should know something soon."

Rachel found herself almost having to bite back a smile. Branson seemed hands off for the most part but the little hidden messages being shot back and forth between them was pretty remarkable.

Once the door was closed, Alberto Spears looked even more frightened. "I'm not talking. I want to call my lawyer."

"Sure," Rachel said. "But again, I have to stress, this does not look good on you, Mr. Spears. The more information you have for us and willingly give us, the better it will be for you later."

"There *is* no later," he said, but his voice was thin and wavering. "I've done nothing wrong."

"Do you know men named Edwin Newkirk or Joseph Staunton?" Rachel asked.

"Or how about Nick Harding and Dustin Adams?"

The constant blinking of his eyes and the inability to keep his hands still told Rachel all she needed to know. Not only was he familiar with the names, but they were making him very uneasy.

"I want to speak with my lawyer."

"Okay," Rachel said. "Have it your way."

She and Jack made their exit, leaving Alberto alone in the interrogation room. Still not familiar with the building, neither of them were sure where to find Branson. As they walked to the bullpen area, an older potbellied officer pointed them to where Branson was seated. He was on the phone when they approached his desk and when he saw them coming, he gave them a smile and held up the *just a second* finger.

"That should do it then," Branson said into the phone. "Thanks for how quick this was." He ended the call, looked to the agents, and said, "The unit that went to Spears's apartment just hit the payload."

"That's good," Rachel said, "because he's still asking for his lawyer."

"Yeah, he's going to need one after this. It seems Alberto Spears works for an up-and-coming cell service provider called PacCall. Neither of the officers that went over there can tell *exactly* what they were looking at, but they're heavily suspecting that he's been tracking or tracing calls. We could get someone on tech to really dive into it, but you're looking at about another twelve hours or so for any real results. But the *real* kicker is that they also found a business card for Better Days Suicide Prevention Hotline on his work desk."

"Yeah, I think that nails him," Rachel said. "It should be more than enough to make him crack, anyway."

"How's that?" Branson asked.

"You said the name of the place was PacCall?"

"Yeah. I'd never even heard of it."

"We can call management to see what Alberto does there," Jack said. "If it happens to be something more than salesman—particularly something with programming the phones—that makes things even more suspicious."

Rachel was already pulling out her phone to Google the business name PacCall. She found it easy enough but had to scroll for a bit to find a contact number for business management. Before she called, she looked to Branson and said: "Let him call his lawyer. If my hunch is right on this, he'll talk to us before a lawyer even gets here. For right now, though, let him think we're being as hospitable as we can be."

Pulling up the number for the PacCall business offices out of Albany, Rachel hurried around the bullpen and to the conference room she and Jack had been using as a makeshift office. It took some of the usual hunting and transferring, but she was finally connected to someone in charge of hiring.

"And you said the man's name was what again?" a woman with a rich northern accent asked.

"Alberto Spears. He lives in Brooklyn."

"And who are you? Why would you need this information?"

"As I told about three people before finally getting in touch with you, my name is Rachel Gift, and I'm a special agent with the FBI. Badge number is JTT 06170056. All I need to know is how long he's been working there, what his job is, and if there have been any disciplinary issues."

"Oh, I see," the woman said. She now seemed helpful as possible, and Rachel could hear the clattering of keys from the other end of the line. "So, I have his record up here. Seems he's been working for us for just under a year. There have been no disciplinary issues at all and from what I can see, he hasn't missed a day or a service call. There's even a note here on his work history where the gentleman who interviewed him for the job marked down 'very promising.' Not sure if that helps or not."

"What's Mr. Spears's job there at PacCall?"

"He's a systems engineer with our New York City division."

"That's exactly what I needed to know," Rachel said. "Thanks so much."

She considered what this all meant and while she could see where it was all trying to lead, she knew they'd need more definitive answers from whatever the officers thought they'd found at the apartment. At the same time, though, she recalled how pale and troubled Alberto had seemed when they'd mentioned the names of the victims. Given that, she felt that if she played her part just right, Albert Spears would willingly give them the information they were looking for. She was just going to have fudge the truth a little.

She met with Jack outside of the conference room and filled him in. When they went back into the interrogation room, Alberto was being escorted back in by Branson. The agents and the detective shared a knowing look as Branson once again closed the door, leaving Rachel and Jack with Alberto.

"Were you able to get in touch with your lawyer?" Jack asked.

"No, but I left a message with his secretary. He's going to return my call within fifteen minutes."

"That's good," Rachel said. "That's *really* good, in fact. Because with what we've just discovered, you're going to need one."

"Sure. You learned so much in the last ten minutes." He was trying to sound confident and tough, but she heard the waver of fear in his voice.

"We did, actually. Can you tell me a bit more about what you do with PacCall? What exactly does an engineer do?"

"Do they know how to patch calls?" Jack asked. "Maybe part of the job is monitoring calls or tracking calls. Does that sound about right?"

"Maybe tracking calls made to Better Days Suicide Prevention Hotline?" Rachel finished.

Little by little, Alberto's eyes grew wider and wider. By the time Rachel dropped the hotline name, he looked absolutely mind-blown. The look on his face reminded her of her own feelings when the tarot reader had revealed her future at the party she and Peter had attended. It sent a little chill through her that she managed to suppress.

"I didn't...I was just..."

And with that, Alberto Spears eyed them both like a child caught in a lie. "They're all dead?"

"Four men," Rachel said. "Yes. All dead."

Alberto's face scrunched up in a tormented expression and he let out a hiss. It was an attempt to keep himself from crying, but it didn't work. Tears came and he slammed his hands down on the table, letting out a shouted curse.

Here we go, Rachel thought. She looked to Jack with expectation and then waited for Alberto Spears to talk.

"Look, I swear, I didn't have anything to do with....with them being *dead.* I thought if they called the hotline, they were better, you know? I just used the fact that they were calling the hotline to sort of bait them."

"Bait them?" Jack asked.

The look that came across Alberto's face was one Rachel had only seen a few times during the course of her career. It was rooted in shame, but it dealt greatly in guilt, too. It was the look of someone who was beginning to realize just how deplorable an action they'd taken part in might be. And in that realization, having to somehow accept it while in the company of strangers.

"All of them had PacCall as service providers. I was sort of tracing calls, about one hundred in all. I was keeping tabs on people who called suicide hotlines. But to keep it simple, I just focused in on one."

"Betters Days Suicide Prevention Hotline," Rachel said.

"But why?" Jack asked. "Did you just call them up to talk shit? To try to make them feel worse about themselves?"

Alberto shook his head. There were still tears coming down his face but Rachel wasn't sure if they were the result of his having been caught or some sort of genuine regret. "I used a voice filter and contacted them. I told them I knew what they were going through. I told them that I would go public with the information unless they paid me. I had recordings of the calls from when I traced them, so I knew all the details. I threatened to put it all online. Their call histories, internet searches on the phone, everything..."

Rachel had heard some pretty awful schemes before, but never anything quite like this. It was so wretched that it took her mind a moment to properly analyze what he was saying. "So you mean to tell me that you were trying to blackmail each of these people, using their suicidal tendencies and thoughts as a payday?"

"Yes."

"Jesus," Jack hissed. "That's low."

"Did it work?" Rachel asked.

"Edwin Newkirk paid five grand. I had another one—Nick Harding—that was setting up a time and place to drop the money off but it never panned out."

The first tear rolled down his face and he lowered his head to wipe it away—as if shedding a few tears was somehow more shameful than what he'd attempted to do.

"Would you be able to provide alibis of where you were for the last several nights?" Rachel asked. She suddenly wanted to be out of the room. If she stayed this close to him for much longer, she was afraid she might say or even do something very stupid and out of line.

"I was at a bar two nights ago. Closed the place down. The only other evidence I'd have is online activity."

Rachel could see him thinking about something…something more than just his whereabouts for the last few nights. She wondered if he was trying to figure out if what he'd just admitted to was an actual crime. The tracing was, for sure. And he'd certainly lose his job once it all came to light.

"Thank you, Mr. Spears." She said this quickly and then hurried out of the interrogation room. Without waiting for Jack, she returned to their makeshift office of a conference room and plopped down in a chair.

In her mind, she placed herself in the shoes of one of the four victims. She tried to imagine what she might have done if she'd gotten a call from a piece of shit like Alberto Spears. What if someone had called her and said: "I'm going to tell everyone about your brain tumor and your suicidal thoughts unless you pay."

It unnerved her. More than that, the idea of it made her furious. For a moment, even the idea of it was too much. She started to feel overwhelmed and as it settled in, a dark cloud rolled along inside of her head. *How much longer do you really think you're going to be able to do this?*

"Hey, are you okay?" came Jack's voice from the door. She turned and saw that he hadn't entered yet, wanting to make sure he gave her some space.

"Yeah, I think so. What he just admitted to…it hit me the wrong way, I think. I mean, that's pretty messed up right?"

"Yes, I'd say so."

"But I do think it pretty much proves that he's not the killer."

"How's that?"

"Well, if he's legitimately trying to blackmail them for money, it doesn't really play to his advantage if they die."

"He could have been lying about the whole blackmail thing."

"I thought about that, too. But he seems smart enough to know what we could easily check up on that. I think he was being mostly truthful about the blackmail aspect. And I think as he voiced it out loud, he started to understand how fucking monstrous it is."

Jack nodded and softly said, "Yeah, I noticed that, too."

"So while he's certainly a real piece of work, he's not our killer."

"We'll need to run those checks on his computer and phone records, but yeah…that's the sense I'm coming to, too."

"So back to nothing more than phone records," Rachel said, exasperated.

"Yeah, but at least that's something."

Rachel simply could not find that optimism. She gathered up the phone records Branson had supplied and started thumbing through them again, though she already felt that she was wasting her time. And behind that lack of motivation, she could still feel that sense of foreboding, wondering how she'd react if someone came forward and tried to blackmail her.

Someone like Alex Lynch, who had already come forward and threatened to play such a hand.

CHAPTER TWENTY

Not content to simply sit around the station, Rachel and Jack headed back out. Four bodies in four nights was a pretty good indicator that a fifth night would end in a fifth body. With no clear leads and all potential suspects ending in dead ends, they decided to head back out to High Bridge over the Harlem River, mainly because it was the most recent crime scene.

Because it was a pedestrian bridge only, it had been closed down. Crime scene tape and heavy sawhorses were stacked at either end. Determined pedestrians (or just those curious about what might have happened on the bridge overnight) could still easily get on if they wanted, but when Rachel stepped out onto it, there were no such brave souls there.

As she walked out onto the bridge, she looked back behind her, down to the same bank the body of Dustin Adams had been pulled out of the night before. Jack was down there, taking pictures and dropping down to his haunches to get a better look at certain areas. She knew that he was once again hung up on the idea that there was something wrong with her. It went beyond his skills of being a good agent and more along the lines of how well he knew her. He was trying quite hard to mind his own business and she respected and thanked him for it, but she could clearly see that it was hard for him.

Rachel walked over to the area where she'd seen the blood the night before, out off the edge of the bridge. It was still there, though harder to see against the metal side because the blood had dried. As she looked out to the water below, she again found herself wondering what that sense of falling might be like. She'd never gone bungee jumping or cliff diving or any nonsense like that, but she figured that sort of jump was one of pure thrill. You knew you were safe, that in the end all was going to be well. But that plunge to certain death had to be something entirely different. She couldn't decide if it made the sensation of falling more thrilling or if it was like a totally separate form of death in and of itself.

The sound of a ringing cell phone broke her from her morbid thoughts. It took two rings for her to realize that it was her phone. She dug it out of her pocket and was surprised to see that it was Peter calling. It was nearing three in the afternoon and it was very much unlike him to call her in the middle of the day...especially if he knew she was out on a case. It made one of her worst fears instantly spring to mind—that something had happened to Paige.

Trying to remain calm but with a hint of caution in her voice, she answered the call. "Hey, Peter. Everything okay?"

"I'm not sure, honestly," he said. "Rach, I just got a really weird phone call."

"Weird how?" she asked. She was legitimately confused now. If it wasn't about Paige, was it maybe about Grandma Tate? Had she called and not made much sense?

"It was a man, and he said he knew you. He said that you were keeping secrets."

Alex Lynch. A plume of hot, white fury sprang up in her. She kept it at bay, though. She had no idea what Alex had said. She was also very much aware that a strange man calling a husband to insinuate that his wife was keeping a secret might make most men think of an affair.

"Did he give a name?"

"No. I asked him a few times and he said he wasn't going to tell. But he said *you'd* know who it was."

"What did he say, exactly?"

"Rachel...what's he talking about? What do you know?"

"I think I know who it might have been, but I need to know what he said."

"He told me that you were keeping secrets from your family. And then he asked me where I thought you'd be in a year."

Rachel gripped her phone and looked back down into the water. She could feel her face growing red with rage and in that moment, she no longer visualized herself plunging to her death into that water, but what it would be like to hold Alex Lynch's head beneath it and feel him down under her grip.

"Rachel, what's going on?" He was concerned, but a little angry, too. She supposed she couldn't really blame him but as the anger flushed through her, she found that she was a little mad at him, too. Did he really think she'd cheat? Did he really think she'd...

What? Keep a secret? Well, yeah...seems you're pretty good at that.

"I don't want you to be alarmed, but yes, I know who it is. His name is Alex Lynch. He's that really deplorable—"

"I remember," Peter said, sounding as if the wind had been taken out of him. "I know who he is. But how the hell did he get my cell phone number, Rachel? And *why* would he get it?"

"I can't give you all the details," she said. "But we had to go to him for a lead on a case and I think it went to his head. He's called me, too."

"Jesus, Rachel. Should I be worried?"

"No. He's in the maximum security wing of a prison. I have no idea how in the hell he got your number, but I'm going to find out."

He sighed on the other end of the line and she could sense the tension in it. She also felt a completely different sort of tension in herself. While she hadn't out and out lied to Peter just now about why she'd met with Alex, she *had* left out the bit about the secret the killer knew about her.

"You good?" she asked.

"I guess. Just…shit, that was spooky. And…there's no secret?"

"No, Peter. It's just him trying to get back at me. I swear I'll look into it."

"Okay. You have to understand, it shook me up, you know? I'm just checking. What about you? Are *you* okay? I know it got under your skin when you had to work that case."

"Yeah, I'm good. Look, I should probably go. This case is going nowhere fast, and I feel like I'm running out of time."

"Okay. Just take care of yourself. Love you."

"You, too," she said, and ended the call.

When she placed the phone back into her pocket, she noticed that Jack was making his way up onto the bridge and heading for her. He was also getting off the phone and he did not look happy. Apparently, it was going to be one of those days.

"What's up?" Rachel asked when he'd closed in, hoping to get him talking about his bad news before he could realize that she'd just been dealt a blow herself.

"I just got a call from the bureau. They let me know that PacCall won't be any help for a few days. Their lawyers are getting pissy about the thing with Alberto Spears and it's going to be like organizing a three-ring circus to get any information from them until it's all cleared up."

"Yeah, that's no good. But really, I think for now we're good. What we have in the phone records we already have is about all we'd need, I think."

"Yeah, until body number five pops up." He shook his head and then, mimicking Rachel from just a few minutes ago, looked down into the Harlem River. "What about you? I saw your face when I started walking your way, just as you put your cell phone away. Looked like you got some pretty bad news yourself."

"Did I?"

"Yeah. Everything okay?"

She didn't answer right away because she could still feel the anger from Alex's call still boiling around inside of her. And if it came out when she spoke, there was no way she would be able to convince Jack that she was fine. So she left her response to a simple nod but even that seemed to be hostile, and she knew it.

"Rachel. Level with me." He paused for a moment, and Rachel could all but see the gears grinding in his head as he tried to decide whether to keep his mouth shut or to go ahead and take that one extra step over the line. In the end, he decided to take the step. "Something's been up with you for the last few weeks. I noticed it during the last case and it's eating at you now, too. You don't owe it to me to tell me, but I think you probably *should* share it."

It pissed her off because she knew he was right. She knew that sharing it with him would take a load off of her heart and it would even be a warm-up for when she had to drop the bomb at home. But at the same time, she knew that if she told him now, right in the middle of a case, it would ruin their work. All of their attention would go toward talking about it and that was the last thing they needed tight now...especially as it felt this case seemed to be more and more elusive with every new body.

"No. It's personal and at the risk of sounding conceited, I don't see that it's affecting my job performance."

"But if you need someone to talk to, even if it might be personal, you can—"

"Didn't we already go through this on the last case? I only need you as a backup and partner while we're on the job. That's it. Nothing else. You're not my shrink, you're not a therapist, and right now, it feels like that's exactly what you're trying to do. So can you just let it go?"

She walked away quickly because she realized even before the eruption was out of her mouth that it was a bit too much. And in knowing that, she felt another emotion rocketing up beyond her anger. She wasn't quite sure if it was guilt or plain old sadness, but she felt tears stinging the corners of her eyes. Before Jack had the chance to make another comment, she hurried away, storming back to the end of the bridge.

When she arrived back at the car, she got behind the wheel and waited. She looked back up to the High Bridge and saw Jack's shape up there. He was walking back to the car, but very slowly. Even then, she knew she should apologize to him but the mere idea of even opening that opportunity up felt too vulnerable. And vulnerability in tandem with the anger and hatred she currently felt toward Alex Lynch's little prank created a very dangerous mix indeed.

Jack took his time getting back to the car; she assumed it was to give them both time to cool down. He didn't look hurt or offended when he got in the car, though his face had taken on an almost stony appearance.

"We need to find a hotel," Jack said. "We both need to rest before this case gets any worse." He did not look at her, keeping his eyes straight ahead on the Harlem River.

"Yeah," was all she said. And though she knew she needed to get some sleep soon, she could also feel the weight of the night on the horizon. They still had a few hours but with the feeling that another murder was almost certain, she didn't want to waste a single moment of daylight.

She started the engine and backed the car away from the bridge. Rachel had no idea what she felt was more pressing: putting a stop to Alex Lynch's little games or committing every bit of her strength to finding this bridge killer. What she did know was that if neither was solved by tomorrow morning, the next few days were going to be incredibly hard.

CHAPTER TWENTY ONE

They got separate rooms located directly beside one another. During check-in and the walk to the rooms, Rachel was acutely aware of the fact that Jack didn't say a single word to her. He didn't so much as glance in her direction as they unlocked their rooms side-by-side. He simply stepped inside and closed his door, leaving Rachel to stew in the knowledge that she'd gone a bit too far when she snapped at him.

She stepped into her room and instantly sat on the edge of the bed. Given the nature of the case, she hadn't even brought her bag in. She doubted she'd be here long. She just needed a quick nap and then she'd head back to the precinct. She took out her phone and called Branson, anxious to already end the call so she could lie back and doze.

"This is Branson," he answered.

"It's Agent Gift. Listen, we've checked into a hotel. We've got to get at least some semblance of rest. But if anything breaks in the next few hours, please give me a call."

"Oh, absolutely. I do have one thing for you. It's not a break per se, because I know you'd suspected it all along, but we just got the results back. The blood from the side of the High Bridge *is* from Dustin Adams. We're still waiting on the finalized coroner's report but the initial findings are leaning heavily towards Adams dying from impact."

"Thanks, Branson. Keep me posted."

She ended the call and kicked her shoes off. She lay back right away, smelling the too-sterile bleach scent of the hotel sheets. Still, sleep came quickly. It was deep and brief, not even broken by the odd dream she had.

In it, Alex Lynch was sitting across from her in an interrogation room. He said nothing to her, but was slapping his right hand over a stack of papers on the table. When she looked down to the table, she saw the papers were medical records—*her* medical records. And each time Alex slapped them, another few pages were added. He began slapping them so hard that his hands started to bleed and his fingers began to tear away from his hand.

She heard this noise in her head when she came awake just thirty-five minutes later. She wasn't quite sure what woke her up; maybe the noise of breaking fingers from her dream, or the distant revving of a motorcycle engine nearby. She closed her eyes to go back to sleep. But her startled mind had already started to reach back out to the facts of the case. And as much as she hated it, she thought of Alex Lynch, too.

She thought of why she'd gone to him in the first place—wanting to try to understand the mindset of a maniacal killer. She wondered if there might be some merit to that here, on this case. Maybe rather than trying to find out the similarities that linked the victims, she needed to try to understand what sort of man would prey on suicidal people. What sort of sick individual would be able to do that four nights in a row? Rachel was no psychiatrist, but she had a good idea that—

"A psychiatrist," Rachel whispered to the room. Then, sitting up and sliding to the edge of the bed, she said it again. "A psychiatrist."

She hurried out of the room and went to the car. She grabbed her folder out of the back seat and sat in the passenger seat, looking through them. Before they'd been cut off from PacCall assistance, the records they'd managed to collect had been helpful. And while it had drawn pretty clear connections between some of the victims, there had been another item found among those blocked phone numbers that had gone overlooked.

One of the blocked numbers had come from a therapist's office. It had seemed rather unremarkable at the time because the number had been on Joseph Staunton's records and he had, after all, been seeing a therapist. She knew there might be hoops to jump through but she figured it might not hurt to speak to the therapist, to see if there was anything Joseph Staunton might have said that either foreshadowed or even predicted what had happened to him. Also, Dustin Adams had been seeing a therapist, too. She couldn't help but wonder if it might have been the same therapist Staunton had been seeing. While she was aware that there had been no blocked numbers leading to a therapist on Adams's records, she also knew that might not mean much. Unless there were calls to set up or schedule appointments, there may never have been any sort of phone contact between them.

It suddenly seemed like a viable lead. She took out her phone and looked through the case notes. She hated to bother a widow during her time of grief, but she needed this information and hoped Mrs. Adams would understand.

The call was answered on the third ring by an older-sounding woman. "Hello? This is the Adams residence."

"This is Special Agent Rachel Gift. I need to speak with Mrs. Adams."

"Are you certain?" the woman asked. "Surely you understand she's dealing with a lot right now."

"Yes, I understand, and I appreciate it. I've already visited her once, so she knows my partner and I are actively trying to figure out if there was foul play involved. I'd like for you to at least tell her I'm on the phone and have just one question for her. If she refuses to speak with me, I'll accept that."

"Fine," the woman said. The amount of vitriol in the woman's voice made Rachel wonder if it was Mrs. Adams's mother. The phone was sat down and Rachel could hear murmuring from the other end. After roughly a minute, it was picked back up and a younger, different voice spoke. It was a ragged voice, worn and tired.

"Agent Gift?" Mrs. Adams said.

"Yes, Mrs. Adams, I'm so sorry to bother you again but I think I may have what could be a potential lead. But I need your help in answering a question. Is that okay?"

"Yes, of course." The woman's voice made it clear that she had not slept yet, that she'd spent the majority of her time in tears ever since her husband died.

"You'd mentioned that Dustin had been seeing a therapist. What was the therapist's name?"

"It was Dr. Pete Deringer. I think I have a card of his somewhere around here if you need the number."

"Yes, that would be helpful. Thank you."

This time, Rachel could tell the phone was being held, carried through the house as Mrs. Adams searched for the business card. "Mrs. Adams, how long had Dustin been seeing Dr. Deringer?"

"About a year. Maybe a tad bit longer." There was a pause, the sound of papers being moved around, and then she said: "Here's the card. Are you ready for the number?"

Rachel took the number down with a pen she plucked from the edge of one of the folders they kept their notes in, jotting it down on the bottom of Joseph Staunton's phone records. She looked to the information Jack had written down while speaking to his contact. She saw that the number Jack had gotten for Staunton's therapist was the exact same number the wife of Dustin Adams had just given her.

It was also listed on Edwin Newkirk's records, as well as Nicholas Harding's.

"Thanks so much for your help," Rachel said.

"Of course. I just...there's no way Dustin killed himself. I don't care *what* it looks like. So please do what you can, and don't hesitate to call me."

When the call was ended, Rachel looked at the phone number. Being that the same number had called both Joseph Staunton and Dustin Adams was a big enough link as far as she was concerned, but she wanted it to be irrefutable. She'd already forced herself to call one grieving family member, so she supposed she may as well act while her determination was pushing her along.

She tried Hannah Newkirk first, but there was no answer. She opted not to leave a message because there was no telling if Hannah would even check her messages for a few days in the wake of all she was dealing with. She then called the number she had for Nick Harding's wife, Amanda. She answered right away and sounded the complete opposite of the Adams widow. She sounded hopeful and almost excited, perhaps hoping the person on the other end may have some answers.

Rachel let her down in that regard, asking her a similar question she'd already asked Mrs. Adams. "Our records show that your husband had been seeing a therapist. Is that correct?"

"Yes," Amanda Harding said, "but he hadn't been in a while. I think his last appointment was around two or three months ago."

"Do you happen to recall the therapist's name?"

"Oh, for sure. Nick raved about him. He said they really hit it off. It was Dr. Wickline. Sam Wickline."

It clearly wasn't a match but there was still one remaining question. If Nicholas Harding had *not* been seeing Peter Deringer, then why was the same blocked number on his records?

"Did he ever deal with a man named Dr. Peter Deringer?"

"No. He found Dr. Wickline and they gelled really well. The only therapist he ever saw was Dr. Wickline."

Rachel could tell that Amanda wanted to go on talking, but she did her best to end the call politely. After all, she now knew that two out of the four victims not only had connections to the same therapist, but had received calls from the therapist's office in the days leading up to their deaths. Also, that same therapist's number was on a third victim's records as well even though there was no apparent link between the two of them. It made no real sense, but that was why it was such an intriguing lead.

That was not just a lead—that was a very strong lead.

First, of course, she needed to try to patch things up with Jack. Because at the end of the day, he'd been right; if they did not work as a unit, the case would suffer. And now, with Dr. Peter Deringer serving as a massive suspect and lead, there wasn't a single second to lose. And if she had to eat some humble pie in order to wrap this case quickly, she was more than willing to do it.

CHAPTER TWENTY TWO

Rachel sat on the edge of Jack's bed, watching as he processed all she'd just told him. She'd not yet attempted an apology or any sort of reconciliation, but had gotten straight to the point. Because when all was said and done, it was the case that truly mattered the most.

"So what you're saying is that at least two of our victims were seeing Dr. Deringer, but at least one of the others was not. But even still, the number is on the phone records of all of the first three victims."

Jack said this all very slowly, trying to properly digest it all as he heard it spoken out loud by his own voice.

"Yes, that's exactly what I'm saying. And if I'm being honest, the part of it that seems the most off-putting is the fact that Deringer's number showed up in Nicholas Harding's phone records even though Deringer never had him as a patient."

"Yeah, that rubs me the wrong way, too. You got an address for Deringer?"

"Not yet. But first…I need to tell you something." It felt as if she had to literally eject the words from her throat; it was much harder than she expected and she wondered what that said about her. "Yes, I'm aware that I have flown off the rails the last few times you've asked me if something is wrong. And I know we covered most of this on the last case we worked and it was pretty much more of the same—me exploding on you because you were showing concern. I understand how unfair that is to you because yes, I absolutely know that it's not you just being nosy. I know that you care and I know you have my back. But, having said all of that, I'm going to ask that you just let me have my privacy for the next several weeks or months. Because the truth of the matter is that I *am* going through something right now. It's something hard and something unexpected, but it's also something that I am in no way ready to discuss with you. Not yet, anyway. And if we're going to work together in an effective capacity, I need you to respect that." She sighed, releasing all of the tension left behind once the words were out. "Are you okay with that?"

He nodded, but she could tell there wasn't much authenticity to it. "I can accept those terms if you can also accept that I *am* going to worry about you. And I hope you know that whatever you're dealing with, I'm here for you. Because you're absolutely right, Rachel. I *do* have your back."

He turned away from her for a moment and slipped his jacket on over his white button-down shirt. "Now, let's go see this doctor. I do have a soft spot for New York City, but I think that's a tourist tendency coming out in me. But really, as the site of a case, it sort of sucks. And I'd love to get out of here as soon as possible."

He started for the door and as his hand fell on the knob, Rachel reached out and lightly grabbed his shoulder. "Jack..."

"Yeah?"

"Are we good?"

He turned to her and the smile he gave her seemed mostly genuine. "Depends. Are you okay? Right now, in this moment, are you okay?"

"Yes," she said. She hated that she wasn't even quite sure if this was true or not.

"Then yes, we're good."

But the way he hurried out the door toward the car made her wonder. She feared that her secrecy had already caused a fissure between them that may never fully heal. So the only pressing question that remained was if they could still work together with that growing divide between them.

***

Dr. Pete Deringer's office was on the third floor of a ten-story building in lower Manhattan. When Rachel and Jack stepped off the elevators, the door to Deringer's offices was just off to the right. The large picture window that looked out into the hallway indicated that Deringer's business took up most of the third floor. When they stepped inside, it was just about what Rachel had expected, only a bit more modern. There were plush couches in the waiting room area, and a gorgeous abstract mural taking up over half of the primary wall. The lighting was low and there was very light music playing from hidden speakers, part soft jazz, part ambient.

Currently, there was no one in the waiting room, which sat off to the left of a slightly curved reception desk. The shape, the lights, and the soft curves of it all made Rachel think of the interior of every spaceship she'd seen in sci-fi movies, sleek and almost futuristic. When they approached the receptionist's desk, Rachel could feel a stirring of excitement between them. The facts of the case so far indicated that

Deringer was a major player in whatever was going on. There was always a certain point in most cases where Rachel could feel the end approaching. She'd always viewed it as going on a long drive and knowing the moment you've taken the last turn that's going to take you to that final destination. She felt some of that now, as she approached the desk.

The receptionist was an almost impossibly attractive brunette who looked to be in her early thirties. She gave them a warm smile that was clearly rehearsed but no less beautiful and reassuring because of it.

"Can I help you?" she asked.

Rachel showed her badge, with Jack doing the same directly behind her. "Special Agents Gift and Rivers," Rachel said. "We need to speak with Dr. Deringer rather urgently."

Rachel watched a flicker of uncertainty pass along the woman's face, which was then quickly replaced by professional caution. "Yes, I see. Okay, well, he's currently with a client and the session won't be over for another twenty-five minutes. I also know that he has another session with another client immediately after that. But if you'll have a seat in the waiting area, I'll make sure to give him your message and he could maybe see you for a few minutes between sessions."

"We just can't wait like that," Jack said. Rachel heard him addressing the receptionist, but her eyes were on the wall behind the desk and slightly to the left. It was, from what she could tell, the only other door in the place other than the two small restroom doors just off the waiting area. "As Agent Gift said, this is rather urgent and we can't waste our time sitting in a waiting area. So, I need you to buzz him or call him or whatever. But we need to see Dr. Deringer *now*."

"I understand that, but I can't allow you to—"

Rachel smiled thinly, gave a little nod, and walked to the door behind the reception area. She did so as if she'd been invited to do so, not running or rushing, and not being brazenly oppositional.

"Ma'am, you can't do that!" the receptionist said.

Completely ignoring her, Rachel reached for the doorknob. She paused, knowing that she was indeed about to cross a line, but wanting to do it in the most moral way possible. Rather than just opening the door and barging in, she knocked. She used her knuckles, giving a loud, pronounced knock.

"Ma'am!" the receptionist hissed, getting to her feet and coming at her in the slowest angry march Rachel had ever seen. "Do you know how—"

Rachel ignored her and knocked a second time, a bit louder this time. Behind her, Jack was speaking to the receptionist, doing a remarkable job of remaining calm and polite.

"We're in the middle of a very time-sensitive case," Jack said. "We've been led to believe that Dr. Deringer can assist in a very big way."

That's putting it lightly, Rachel thought. She had raised her hand to knock a third time when it was finally answered. It opened rather quickly and she found herself looking at a roguishly handsome man that she guessed to be in his early fifties. His salt and pepper hair was thick, and his face was clean-shaven. His pronounced jaw and brow made his face looked as if it had been chiseled out of marble. He was doing his absolute best to look as if he were cool and collected, but Rachel could see his irritation in the taut muscles of his face.

He looked from Rachel to his receptionist, standing behind her and just off to the right. His eyes again settled on Rachel and he asked: "Can I help you?"

"You can, actually," Rachel said, showing him her badge. "We're working on a very time-sensitive case and need to speak with you."

"And it can't wait another twenty minutes?"

"We can't be sure of that. And quite frankly, we didn't see the point in just wasting time. You *are* Dr. Pete Deringer, correct?"

"Yes," he said, eying the badge closer this time. "What is the case?"

"We'll tell you in your office, just the three of us."

Still clearly annoyed, Deringer gave a curt nod, so quick and snappy that a bystander might have thought he had a pinched muscle in his neck. "One moment, please."

Deringer shut the door and Rachel could just barely hear him speaking to whoever was inside. Rachel then noticed that the receptionist had slowly started making her way back to her seat. She kept her eyes on them, though, her expression making it look like she'd been nearly traumatized by their bullying. Rachel felt the slightest ping of regret but she didn't have time to examine it. She was at the point where she was willing to do just about anything to get to the bottom of this case. She'd be damned if she was going to allow time to slip away so easily when there was a potential fifth victim lurking around the corner.

She and Jack remained at their place by Deringer's office door until it opened again about three minutes later. Deringer escorted a patient out—an older man wearing a flannel shirt and ripped jeans—and the receptionist began chatting with him about setting up a make-up appointment.

"Come on in, then," Deringer said. "Not that I really had much of a choice."

He walked to his desk, leaned against it, and crossed his arms. Rachel could see the smug look on his face right away and she knew this was not going to be easy. Though he was not a large man, he had the look of someone who was not going to be moved, no matter what.

"I certainly hope this *is* a very important matter because you just disrupted a session with a client I've been working with for over a year. Not that you'd care, but he'd showing great progress and you just ruined a potential breakthrough. So…what's so damned important?"

"Dr. Deringer," Rachel said, "did you know that two of your clients have recently died?"

"What?" The shock on his face was apparent. He went through a few different emotions, from confusion to alarm; she supposed he might have thought he'd misunderstood them at first.

"Joseph Staunton and Dustin Adams. They've both died in the last three days, both from what appear to be suicides by jumping from bridges."

"Suicides?" he asked. His eyes squinted a bit, and he looked like a man who was slowly getting lost in very deep thought. "I don't…I don't see how that's possible. Especially not with Dustin. I don't know how…"

"While these deaths are obviously unfortunate," Jack added, "the more interesting thing is that a blocked number called each of them in the two days leading up to their deaths. We had some folks at the FBI look into it and the number that was being blocked ended up being *your* number. Your office number, to be exact."

"Dr. Deringer, if you were to call my cell phone right now, would it show up as unlisted?"

"No." He said this with a cruel tension. It was evident that he could see where this line of questioning was headed and he wanted to cut it off at the knees. "And before you make any accusations that would make you sound foolish and maybe even get you in some deep, heated water with your direct supervisor, let me tell you right now that I run a very tight ship. Any alleged calls to these men that came from here were for appointment purposes only."

"Even when the calls are being somehow blocked?"

Rachel was a bit surprised when Deringer took an offensive step toward them. For just a brief moment, she was pretty sure she saw an arrogant smirk touch the corners of his mouth. "If you're here to accuse me of something, go ahead and do it."

"Okay," Rachel said. "What about Edwin Newkirk and Nick Harding? You have clients by those names?"

Without pause, Deringer responded, "You ever hear of doctor-patient confidentiality?"

Jack met his one step, closing the distance between them even closer. "I have. Have *you* heard of reasonable suspicion or probable cause?"

This time, Deringer's smile was a little plainer to see. "I have. And this has been a pleasant chat, but you've already interfered with one of my clients today. I'd appreciate it if you'd get out of here and allow me to prepare for my next one."

"Dr. Deringer, two of your clients have died, allegedly of their own doing," Rachel said. "Doesn't that upset you?"

"Of course it does. It upsets me even more than two entitled FBI agents barging into my office and accusing me of…well, of what? I don't know. Because you haven't been very clear on that. Now, if you want to accuse me of something or get access to my phone records, I suggest you go on and get a warrant."

"Oh, if you need us to be clear, we can," Rachel said. She looked over to Jack and said, "How clear should we be?"

"Dr. Deringer," Jack said, closing the distance between them and taking out his handcuffs. "You're under arrest for suspected involvement in the deaths of Edwin Newkirk, Joseph Staunton, Nick Harding, and Dustin Adams."

As Jack spun Dr. Deringer around to get his wrists, the therapist fought for just a bit. When Jack pulled his arm hard behind his back, Deringer let out a shout of pain and then stopped. When Jack turned him back around, Deringer was livid. If looks could kill, Rachel figured she and Jack would have dropped dead right then and there.

"I'm not sure why you look so upset," Rachel said. "You asked us to be clear. And now you get to be clear with us from the comfort an interrogation room."

Deringer did not protest this, but the angered expression on his face told Rachel that it was taking great restraint for him to remain quiet. He remained that way, wordless and grudgingly cooperative, as the agents escorted him out of the office, through the polished waiting area, and right by the alarmed receptionist.

CHAPTER TWENTY THREE

Rachel had to hand it to Dr. Pete Deringer. He really did seem to be that immovable force he'd positioned himself as back at his office. Even when he was in an interrogation room and was clearly uncomfortable with his surroundings, he remained just as stubborn as ever. His attitude threw Rachel off a bit, though. He was displaying the sort of stubbornness she'd often seen in men who were playing along because they *knew* they were innocent and just wanting the FBI to screw up royally so they could use it against the bureau, looking to sue or find some other advantageous play. She got some of that from Deringer, but she also sensed something different.

First of all, if this man was a respected therapist, it seemed to Rachel that he'd be bending over backwards to make sure he could help find the reasons that two of his clients were dead. If they were legitimate suicides, surely he'd want to be looking into solutions for damage control. Instead, he showed little to no remorse over their deaths and seemed more concerned with making some kind of a point. Rachel couldn't quite pin down any specific motive, though, and it was starting to irritate her.

Deringer had been sitting in the room for ten minutes, still not speaking. He sat behind a metal table, the room smelling like cleaning solution and strong black coffee. When Rachel and Jack came into the room, he gave them that same arrogant smile (a smile that was making Rachel want to punch him in the teeth more and more every time she saw it) and folded his hands on the table.

"Get that warrant yet?" he asked.

"Working on it," Jack said.

"Dr. Deringer, things escalated so quickly back at your office that we never even got to mention the most damning piece of evidence of all."

"This should be good." Deringer smirked. "I've done nothing wrong. And if you're trying to suggest that I had something to do with the deaths of those two men, I'm actually rather anxious to hear the story behind it."

"I'm glad you said that," Rachel said. She placed several copied printouts on the table in front of him. They were portions of the phone records that had been collected so far. Before coming into the room, Rachel had circled the blocked or unlisted number on each of the records. The final printout was from an email the bureau had sent Jack, showing the actual number that had been hidden behind whatever blocked device or method had been used to keep the number private.

"As I said, your number popped up on the records of two of your patients within forty-eight hours of their deaths," she said. "That would be Dustin Adams and Joseph Staunton. But what's really striking us as odd is why anyone from your office would have called Nicholas Harding or Edwin Newkirk. I know for a fact that Harding wasn't seeing you. He was seeing a man named Wickline. But this blocked number, which the bureau cracked to discover is your office number, called them. You claim calls to Adams and Staunton would have been for appointments. So why would you call men that you weren't even doing business with?"

"And for that matter," Jack asked, "how would you even know *to* call them? How could you have possibly known they'd been having issues that resulted in them visiting therapists?"

For the first time since they'd come face-to-face with Deringer, he looked off his game. He eyed them both, trying to gauge the moment, perhaps to see if there was any remaining ammunition coming his way.

"I'd like to call my lawyer," Deringer said. And in that plea, Rachel heard the first true signs of worry. Mentioning the two men who had not been his patients seemed to have flustered him.

Rachel had been in this position before—more times than she could count. Deringer was the typical specimen that always presented as tough-willed and in control when they first met. But the moment a piece of evidence was presented that they feared they could not get around, they buckled a bit. The aforementioned evidence alone was not enough to get them to break. That took a little extra nudge, a nudge that was most effective when presented from a sympathetic stance.

"That's fine," Rachel said. "We'll give you the call. But before we do, I feel I should let you know every aspect of this case."

"No, I want my—"

"Four men have died in the last four days. One man each night. They are dying in what look to be suicides by jumping from bridges, but at least two of them seem to have some sort of foul play involved. We know that two of them were your patients and yes, the fact that you called the two others despite them never having worked with you makes things look pretty bad on your end. However...four men in four nights pretty much has us expecting a fifth man tonight—on the fifth night. If you know *anything*, you can help bring the killer to justice. You can help us find him."

She was rather proud of the trap she'd set. Based on his response, he could very well inadvertently admit to being the killer. But within seconds, the expression on his face had her worried that was not going to be the case.

"You should also know," Jack said, "that we'll have that warrant within an hour or so. It usually takes longer but we're dealing with a potential serial killer here, so it'll get pushed through quickly. If we get that warrant before your lawyer gets here, he won't be able to protect you from our searches. So, if there's anything you need to tell us before we go to your office and find out for ourselves, I suggest you do it now. It'll look much better on you in the end."

Rachel could see Deringer calculating his next move. She had no doubt that he was a clever man and that the requirements of his job would likely have had him come across certain laws about rights and securities pertaining to this very situation. Slowly, he leaned forward. When he spoke, his voice was softer than it had been since he'd first opened his office door to Rachel.

"I did not have anything to do with those deaths. When you get your warrant and search my office and phone records, you'll see that I was telling you the truth about Dustin Adams and Joseph Staunton."

"And what about the others?"

Deringer shook his head, but not out of stubbornness. He was fighting with himself, the shaking of his head coming in the realization of something. It was yet another thing Rachel had seen on many people who started out strong-willed and slowly crumpled when confronted with damning evidence.

"I never actually spoke to Newkirk. He hung up on me right away."

"So you did call him?" Rachel asked.

"Yes." He breathed heavily a few times and stared at his still-clasped hands. "I called Edwin Newkirk and Nicholas Harding. They were not patients. I got their numbers through a man I hired."

"I don't follow," Jack said. "What sort of man? Hired for what?"

"I had a man monitoring three local suicide hotlines. It's apparently quite easy when the calls are made with cell phones. It's not hacking, I don't think...not really. But he was able to supply me with the phone numbers and, in some cases, the names of people who were calling these hotlines. I'd wait a day or so and then call them, presenting myself formally and asking if they were currently seeing a therapist or speaking with a professional about their issues."

The reality of what this meant slowly settled on Rachel but even then, she had to be sure she was understanding him correctly. "So, you mean you were headhunting new patients?"

"Yes." When he looked back up to them, some of that stubbornness was back in his features. "I know it seems unethical, but it's not all that uncommon."

"Which part?" Jack asked. "Calling depressed people and trying to drum up business or paying someone to hack a few phone lines?"

Deringer started shaking his head again and his eyes were once more on his clasped hands.

"Can you give us proof of your whereabouts for the last few nights?" Rachel asked. "Specifically between the hours of eleven and three in the morning?"

"I was at home, sleeping."

"Any proof?"

"No. I live alone and don't go out much. Maybe here and there on the weekend and...you know what? No. I'm done for now. I've told you the truth. And now I want my lawyer."

"You sure that's the truth?" Rachel asked. "The *entire* truth?"

"I did *not* have a hand in killing those men!"

"Not even calling them up and goading them into jumping?" Jack asked.

"God, no! Why the hell would I do that?" He looked somewhere between angry and terrified when he added: "I mean, think about it. Why would I want to kill them if I was trying to net them as new patients?"

Rachel thought she might believe him, but it was hard to sort out of her own feelings in that moment. Maybe it was because she was so close to death's door that she was blinded by a strange sort of fury. This was now two men who had admitted to trying to profit from the misery and mental anguish of others. It was one of those instances where the sheer evil of people was a little too plain to see and it made it hard to really give a damn about who was innocent and who was guilty.

"We'll send someone in to make sure you can call your lawyer," Rachel said, heading for the door. "We'll see you again after the warrant clears and we've had a look at your office and phone records."

She hesitated for a moment because it looked like Deringer was on the verge of saying something else. In the end, though, he remained quiet. She was essentially fine with this, as the warrant would allow them to get whatever answers they needed. She and Jack left the room and when she closed the door behind them, she immediately felt the pressure of the case. She checked her watch and saw that it was 3:21. The night was quickly approaching—approaching so quickly that she could barely recall where the day had gone.

"What do you think?" Jack asked as they headed out in search of Branson or one of the assistant officers to escort Deringer to a phone. "It seems to fit, right?"

"It does, on the surface," she admitted. "But his alibi might prove that he's at least partially truthful."

"What? Being at home all four nights?"

"I mean the story about hiring someone to tap into those phones. Once we get that warrant, I imagine such a thing would be easy to find. And if it turns out that his story about that *terrible* little operation is true, then I think it does cast a shaky light on his potential guilt."

"You don't think he might have just gotten pissed that someone turned down his offer to help them—for a fee? I mean, based on what he was trying to do to drum up business, he's not exactly a moral man."

"Maybe. But then, why kill off clients? If he's calling these non-clients for new business, what sense does it make that he would kill current clients?"

Harsh understanding came across Jack's face. "Yeah, that *is* a good point."

They came to Branson's desk, near the back of the bullpen, and saw that he was on his desk's landline phone. He beckoned them over just as he was setting the receiver back down into its cradle.

"Did you get anything out of him?" Branson asked.

"A bit," Rachel said. "But I don't know that it's going to turn out to be anything worth a damn."

"If it helps, that was the magistrate I was on the phone with. He says the warrant will be good to go in about fifteen minutes. So as far as I'm concerned, that means we can start searching. What do you need from me?"

"As much manpower as you can lend to look his business and apartment over. We're also going to need someone from tech to get into his phone and laptop as quickly as possible."

"Anything else?"

"Yeah," Jack said. "Get someone to walk him to a phone. He keeps asking to speak to his lawyer. And with what he's already told us, I really feel like he's going to need it."

CHAPTER TWENTY FOUR

The gorgeous receptionist back at Deringer's office somehow managed to still look immaculate despite her angry stare. The stare was mostly directed at Rachel, even though there were two NYPD officers and Jack accompanying her. One of the officers was straight from the technical department. While Rachel, Jack, and the officer looked through some of the papers on and in Deringer's desk, the technician was on the phone with someone else, cooperatively walking through the process of tapping into the laptop of Deringer's desk. Rachel also got the impression that the person on the other end of the line was at the station, doing the very same thing to the cell phone they'd taken from Deringer's possession when he'd been processed.

Feeling confident that any clues or leads would come from a digital means, Rachel felt almost useless in looking through the scattered papers. More than that, she also knew that if they weren't careful with things like personal records and client histories in a therapist's office, it could very well come back to bite them in the ass.

Given these things, she turned her attention back to the receptionist. She was standing just outside of Deringer's office door with her arms folded and a smoldering look on her face. Honestly, it perfectly echoed Deringer's exact attitude when they'd first spoken with him. When Rachel walked over to her, the receptionist backed away a bit. When she realized Rachel intended to speak with her, the receptionist stopped when she reached her desk, choosing to stand by the side and try to hold her own.

"Were you aware that Dr. Deringer was having someone illegally tap into phone lines to get names and numbers from suicide hotlines?"

The woman looked as if someone had just told her the world was flat and the oceans were filled with talking dinosaurs. "What on earth are you talking about?"

"He admitted it to it himself in interrogation," Rachel said. "Did you have no idea about it?"

"No," she said, her voice little more than a whisper. "I had absolutely no idea."

"Was he secretive?" Rachel. "Did you ever notice him making sure to close his office door even when not in session? Or maybe he took a lot of private calls that weren't related to work?"

"I don't know about the calls. But I mean, he always had his door closed. It's just something he's always done, even when he's not with a client. I figured it was just the way he preferred to work. Even when there are no clients in there, there's always a ton of paperwork."

Taking a shot in the dark, Rachel went another way. "By any chance, can you recall Dustin Adams and Joseph Staunton?"

"I recognize both names, sure. But I knew Joseph quite well. He had gotten so that he was very chatty with me, very friendly. It was the polar opposite of how he was when he started seeing Dr. Deringer. Even I could see vast improvements from my limited interactions with him."

"How about—" she started, but a shout from the office interrupted her.

"Agents," said the technician currently sitting behind Deringer's laptop. "Officer Holmes down at the precinct has something for us."

Rachel hurried back into the office, where everyone was huddled around Deringer's large desk. The technician was placing his phone down on the desk and clicking around on the laptop. "He's going to conference call us on this laptop so we can all hear it," he explained.

"Hear what, exactly?" Jack asked.

"He says there's a voicemail on Deringer's phone and the source appears to be from Edwin Newkirk."

As soon as he said this, the noise of a FaceTime call came over Deringer's laptop. The technician answered and they all found themselves looking at the pale, waifish face of Officer Holmes. He was perched behind two laptops, and a desktop monitor sat off to his left.

"Okay, Holmes, we have you on," the technician said. "What have you got?"

"There's a voicemail message to Pete Deringer from Edwin Newkirk," Holmes said. "It was received five days ago. Hold on one second and I'll play it for you. I've got it hooked up so you should all be able to hear it pretty clearly."

As they waited, Rachel was reminded of the moment back at Better Days Hotline offices, siting with Lisa and Shelby and listening to the call recordings. It only intensified when Edwin Newkirk's voice came through Deringer's laptop speakers.

"Dr. Deringer, this is Edwin Newkirk and I'm going to tell you just this one time. If you ever call me again, I'm going to report you. I don't know how you got my number or how you know I've been in therapy, but the idea of finding a new patient on the phone seems very impersonal and I'm insulted, quite frankly. So consider this your first and last warning. Don't even *think* about calling me again."

The click to end the call was quite audible, even through the laptop's small speakers.

"Is that it?" Rachel asked.

"Yeah, that's all I've got on my end so far," Holmes said.

"When was that message left?"

"It's logged as coming in five days ago at two-oh-five in the afternoon."

Without the records in front of her, Rachel did her best to recall the dates the unblocked numbers had come to the phones of the victims. She was quite sure the number that had eventually turned out to belong to Deringer had been made to Edwin Newkirk six days ago. So the call from Edwin would have come *after* the incoming call from the blocked number. In other words, the timeline made sense. But then again, the timeline also supported Jack's thin theory that Deringer could have gotten upset about being rejected and then acted out.

"Thanks, Holmes," the technician said. "Ping me if there's anything else." With that, he ended the conference call and looked awkwardly at the laptop. "As for the laptop," he said, looking at Rachel and Jack, "it's all records and notes from client sessions. And I'm sure I don't have to tell you about the pile of mess we'd get into if we went looking through all of that unless we were one hundred percent, absolutely certain Deringer was our guy."

"Hell, I don't know that I'd do it even then," Jack commented.

"So where does that leave us?" the technician asked. "Should I keep looking anyway? If Deringer is involved in this, we need to know for sure by nightfall."

Rachel nodded, feeling oddly reassured that even the NYPD were part of the unspoken understanding that it was all but expected for a fifth body to show up tonight if they didn't have the actual killer in custody.

"His alibis are paper thin," Jack said. "And I know this message from Newkirk backs up Deringer's story about the headhunting-clients thing, but I think it also points pretty hard to him being a very likely suspect."

"I think that's the overall verdict around the station, too," the other officer said.

Rachel completely understood how it could be seen this way but it just didn't sit right with her. "All the same, I'd like to keep looking. As soon as his lawyer arrives, Branson is welcome to question him all he likes. But we can't just sit around and assume we have our guy only to end up with another dead body on our hands."

She got two nods of respect from the officers and a knowing grin from Jack. He turned to the officers and said, "You guys good with that?"

"Yeah, sounds good to me," the tech said.

Rachel and Jack made their way out of the office, bypassing a now frazzled-looking receptionist who would likely be doing little more than answering phone calls from confused and concerned clients for the next few days.

"Any new ideas where to look?" Jack asked as they made their way back into the hallway.

"Nothing new," she said. And with her mind once again turning to the phone records that had, so far, provided plenty of fruit, she said: "I was thinking there might still be something to find in the old ideas."

CHAPTER TWENTY FIVE

When they pick up the phone, they imagine this must be the feeling an alcoholic gets when touching the first bottle of the night. There was a thrill of anticipation and the absolute certainty of how the night was going to go. Picking up the new burner phone was like picking up that first bottle. Punching in the numbers was popping the top off the bottle. And when the phone rang on the other end, that was the first delicious sip.

The clock on the wall read 5:47. The timing had to be right. It had taken some time, some trial and error, to figure it out exactly, but they were confident now. And they'd done this enough in the past to know the right words to say, how to sway a mood or a mind that seemed already to be set on one course.

The phone rang twice and was answered by a man with a thin, uncertain voice. "Hello?" he asked with suspicion and annoyance, which was typical of someone answering their phone to an unknown number in this age of telemarketer assaults.

They responded quickly, wanting them to hear a real, authentic voice. A comforting voice, a voice that cared.

"Hello. I'm looking for Paul Vance."

"Yeah, this is him."

"Paul, please forgive the abrupt nature of this call, but I was told you were in a particularly bad place. I was told you may need some help."

There was a pause on the other end and then, as they'd expected, an almost angry response. But it was an anger rooted in hope. "Yeah, and who the hell told you that?"

"That's not important. What's important is that I can help you. I can help you like I've helped so many others."

"Is this some religious bullshit?"

They couldn't suppress their laughter. "No. But I suppose you *could* say I've been sent. At least, that's how I feel. Paul, I can help you. If you let me, I can help."

Another pause and then, "Did Harry put you up to this? Seriously, who is this?"

Again, as the last word came to an end, they could hear that little inflection of hope in Paul Vance's voice.

"You'll find out later, I'm sure," they answered. "The important thing right now is that I know you. Paul Vance, forty-eight years of age. Your marriage is in shambles, you hate your job, and you tried to kill yourself four months ago."

"How do you kn—"

"It doesn't matter for now, Paul. You need someone, right? Someone to help you? Someone to be there for you. Would you meet with me?"

"No. I don't know how you know all of this about me, but I could call the cops. I could…this is a crime."

It was like a blueprint. Every other time, this conversation had gone down this same path, taking these same exact turns. And because of that, they knew what came next. They knew it was almost done now.

"You could do that, yes. Absolutely. But that would heap just one more thing on you and really…do you want that? You need a break. You need someone that will listen. I do that and I do it well."

"Are you some sort of doctor?" Paul Vance asked.

"No. I can be better than a doctor. Meet me, Paul. Meet me and you can find out who I am, how I know these things about you, and how I can help. Really, don't you deserve someone that will actually listen? Someone that will care? I know how alone you feel and I know how that can eat away at someone."

It was hard to be sure, but they thought Paul might actually be crying on the other end of the phone. And in that sound of breaking, they knew what came next. It just took a while for the person on the other end to finally get there. With Paul Vance, the silence went on for another fifteen seconds or so.

"Yes. I'll meet you. But if this is some sort of trick, I'll—"

"No trick, Paul. You have my word on that. You'll see."

"Where do I need to meet you?"

They gripped the phone, and now it was like that sixth or seventh beer going down, the real buzz just beginning. And with that feeling rushing through them, they told Paul Vance where and when to meet.

CHAPTER TWENTY SIX

Night fell like a stained shroud over New York City and as she looked out the windshield of the rental car, Rachel felt as if she were suffocating. The last little remnants of daylight struggled in a golden ribbon along the Hudson River and behind countless buildings, but the night squashed it out. Rachel and Jack had opted to be out on the streets, already making the circuits between potential suicide bridges. Jack held the phone records and every little note they'd made along the way and Rachel could tell that he was doing all he could to not come out and say the obvious. In the end he simply couldn't keep it in, though.

"We've gone over everything," he said. "There's the one final blocked number that we currently can't break because of PacCall's lawyers tying everything up. Which, honestly, is utter bullshit."

"If we really press that Pete Deringer is our guy, that blocked number could come back to look bad on us," Rachel pointed out. "What happens if three weeks down the road we find out the location and caller and it completely reveals Deringer's innocence?"

"Then we're screwed," Jack said. "But I think it's almost forgivable, given the way things are currently looking for Deringer *and* the fact that it's the only strong lead we have."

"I don't like it," Rachel said. "Something doesn't fit and—"

Jack's cell phone rang, interrupting her. He answered it, placing the call on speaker mode. "This is Agent Rivers."

"Rivers, it's Branson. Look, Deringer's lawyer has been here for the past hour and ever since then, Deringer has been giving us everything we're asking for. He can tell us everything about the last four nights right down to what he had for dinner. After some back and forth and guilt, he did reveal that he visited a porn website on his phone three nights ago just a little shy of midnight."

"Even if we can prove that with his phone's activity history, it's not going to completely rule him out at the site of the murder."

"Yeah, I know. I've got the tech guys working with the phone company to see if they can get a read on the location of his phone over the past four days, but that won't be concrete either. He could have just left it at home."

"Seems doubtful, though," Jack said. "If he's using his phone to reach out and stay in touch with the people he was trying to snatch up, you'd think he'd have his phone on him."

"Yeah, that idea has been bounced around here, too," Branson said. "What I'm getting at is now that the lawyer is here, Deringer is being pretty damned forthcoming. It may not be a bad idea for the two of you to come back if there's anything specific you want to know. But based on what we're getting from him, it might very well be a waste of your time."

"And yours," Rachel said. "Branson, I know it's inconvenient, but we're going to need the same set-up we had last night. I need as many as you can send out to every bridge you can think of."

"I'm already setting all of that up on my end, but I can tell you right now that we're not going to get the same manpower he had last night. Half the people in this station think Deringer is the guy—it's just a matter of finding the smoking gun. And the ones who matter, including my captain, are the main ones who are buying that line of thought. It also doesn't help that despite so many officers being committed to it last night, we still ended up with Victim Number Four."

"Yeah, I figured that was going to happen," Rachel said, not bothering to hide the irritation in her voice. She did understand the train of thought behind this approach but wasn't ready to put all her chips on Deringer just yet. She wondered what the reaction to that specific train of thought would be tomorrow morning if there was a Victim Number Five.

"I'll keep you posted on happenings around here, and the first groups will head out to keep an eye on bridges in the next hour or so."

They ended the call as Rachel looked out into the night, the Brooklyn Bridge standing out against the natural dark. The fact that there were twenty-one bridges just in Manhattan was mind-boggling—and they already knew their killer wasn't working specifically in the Manhattan area. She knew there were roughly two thousand bridges and tunnels in all of New York City combined, and bridges with any considerable height that might be a fitting site for a suicide numbered in the high five hundreds. In other words, even if the NYPD threw dozens more units at this case, they were still basically looking for a needle in a haystack.

She also couldn't help but wonder if the one remaining blocked number they could not get access to might be the needle. And if so, if it was going to end up sticking them in a deadly fashion.

"If a fifth person dies tonight, this is going to become a media circus," she said, really just thinking out loud. "And I don't even want to know how Anderson would react."

"So what could we possibly be missing?" Jack asked, slapping at the papers in his lap.

Her mind was racing and when her cell phone rang, she almost resented it. Even if it was Branson with more updates on Deringer, she sensed that it would be nothing of any real use. When she saw that it was a FaceTime call from Peter, her mind stopped racing and, instead, seemed to trace backward. She thought of the last two times she'd spoken with him. The first time, he'd told her how he'd screwed up and accidentally let it slip to Paige that Grandma Tate was sick and was going to die; the last time, he'd been freaked out because Alex Lynch had called him, teasing him with a secret his wife was keeping.

"Need to pull over for privacy?" Jack asked. "I can hop out for a moment."

"No, that's fine." She'd already decided that she'd not paint a pretty picture for Peter. She and Jack were under a ton of pressure and every now and then, Peter needed to be aware of things like that. Besides, based on the last two conversations they'd had, she wasn't sure she could handle more upsetting news from home.

She answered the call, setting the phone in the console cup holder and angling it toward her face. When she saw Paige's face rather than Peter's, she couldn't help but smile. From the looks of it, Paige had just gotten out of the shower. Her wet hair was dripping onto her Pokémon pajamas.

"Mommy!"

"Well, hey there, squirt. How are you?"

"I'm good. But I can barely see you!"

Jack chuckled from the passenger seat. He picked up Rachel's phone and held it out toward her so that Paige could see her mother.

"Better?" Rachel asked.

"Yeah! Hey, you're driving! I didn't think you were supposed to drive and talk on the phone."

"Mr. Jack is holding the phone for me."

"Oh. Hi, Mr. Jack!"

"Hey, Paige. Long time no see."

Rachel tried to recall the last time Jack had seen her family. She thought it had been sometime around last Christmas at a party Jack had thrown at his apartment. "Hey, Paige," Rachel said, "is Daddy around?"

"Yeah, he's sitting right here."

"Hey, babe," Peter said in the background. "And hey, Jack!"

"Good. I need you both to hear this. This is one of those times where it's really not a very good time to talk. You know I love you, though, right?"

"Right," Paige said, clearly saddened. But then she cheered up and when she smiled, she said: "Are you chasing after a bad guy *right now*?"

"Not quite. But look, I do need to go, okay? I'll make it up to you by calling tomorrow."

"Do you know when you'll be home?" Paige asked.

"Not yet. But maybe I can let you know before you leave for school in the morning. How's that sound?"

"Okay. G'night, Mommy. Love you!"

"I love you, too." She then raised her voice a bit and added: "And you, too, Peter!"

Jack ended the call and set the phone back into the console. "That girl might be *too* cute," he said. "I don't know how you can stand it."

"It takes practice, that's for sure."

They'd come to a red light and it then occurred to Rachel that they could literally drive all night, going to every bridge they happened to pass by and not put a scratch in the number of places they could possibly go. They had no leads, no clues, no idea as to where they should even start.

"So is she just super well-behaved or are you that good of a mother?" Jack asked.

Yanked out of her despair, Rachel jerked a bit, almost having missed what he'd said. "What do you mean?"

"You told her you couldn't talk as sweetly and as rationally as you could and she was fine with it. She understood. That's pretty cool."

"Yeah, I guess it *is* pretty cool. She'd always been really good at understanding things like that, though. Rationalizing things like that with a kid her age isn't easy. It takes a lot of practice."

The light turned green and as she passed through it, the comment that had just come out of her mouth seemed to catch on something in her mind. *Rationalizing things…it takes a lot of practice.*

Then, almost as an afterthought and not part of her conversation with Jack at all, she added: "You really have to know how to talk to someone…"

"What?" Jack asked.

126

"Something just occurred to me. That one last number that we don't have an identity for...would you say it's a safe bet that the caller knew the four men had once had suicidal tendencies?"

"I think they at least knew they'd been having issues. Maybe even that they'd been to therapy."

"So the caller would have to know something along those lines. But they'd also need to have their number. Which, thanks to our suspects so far, we know isn't very hard to do. Deringer hired someone to do it and Alberto Spears knew how to do it himself. So really, all three people we've questioned all had access to these men's names, their history of depression and/or suicidal thoughts, and their phone numbers. And of all three of our suspects so far, there's only been one who would have access to those things without any outside help."

"You mean Lisa at Better Days."

"Yes."

"But she checked out. She's clean...right?"

Rachel considered it for a minute. "Is she?" Her mind started to take a turn it had shied away from at first but as she started speaking the idea out loud, it started to make a dark sort of sense.

"Let's assume, just for the sake of argument, that the scene where there were no signs of foul play were *actual* suicides," she went on. "Let's say the caller contacted them and talked them into it somehow. But with the other two, the caller's words weren't quite enough. They had to give an extra bit of effort and met with them...maybe even pushed them."

"It's plausible, but feels like a stretch."

"Oh, for sure. But *what if?* What if the killer was there at the scene for the first two. Maybe just watching. And if either Nick Harding or Joseph Staunton had changed their minds at the last minute, the killer would have been there to make sure it was done." As she said these things out loud, something in her gut told her she was on to something. And the more she thought about it, the more foolish she felt for letting Lisa so easily off the hook.

"So the big question remains: *why?*" Jack asked.

"No clue. Based on some of the other reasons we've gotten for getting the numbers of suicidal people during this case, I'm nearly afraid to ask. But I do know this...if someone was going to talk a suicidal person into going through with it, who better than someone who has been trained to talk them *out* of it?"

They'd come to another red light and traffic was getting thicker. She looked at Jack and saw that a faint dawning sort of expression had come over his face. He wasn't completely sold on her idea yet, but it had hooked him. "I think it warrants at least another discussion with her," he said. "It's not like we're drowning in leads anyway."

With the light still red, Rachel pulled up Shelby's personal number. She answered right away and Rachel matched her urgency, wasting no time.

"Shelby, is Lisa on shift right now?"

"No, she's not due to come in until midnight."

It felt a little off, as two of the four victims had been killed after midnight, but it was still worth looking into. And they didn't have time to sit down with Lisa's schedule to compare it with the times of each victim's death.

In front of Rachel, the light turned green and she pressed on. Gripping the phone in determination, she said: "Then if you have it, I'm going to need her home address."

CHAPTER TWENTY SEVEN

The address Shelby gave them was a fifteen-minute drive from where Rachel had made the call. Add with traffic and a driver unfamiliar with the city, it took closer to twenty-five. Lisa lived in a ten-story apartment on the corner of a fairly busy intersection, and they were able to find a parking spot a block over. As they walked to the building, Rachel checked her watch and saw that it had somehow come to be 9:57. It seemed that once night had fallen over the city, it had also started eating away their time. The late hour made Rachel feel as if the night were actually chasing them; after all, if they did not find the actual killer before the sun came up, she was certain there would be a fifth body. So, if the night was indeed chasing them, it was a race Rachel intended to win.

The apartment building was a classic sort of clean—not a place someone would consider run-down and dirty, but not the crowning achievement of cleanliness and sophistication either. Lisa resided in Apartment 221, so they took the stairs to the second floor. As they walked down the hall, the sounds of a typical apartment at night greeted them: scattered and muted conversations, the soft hum of television shows and music, the ambient drone of the building's air conditioning.

When they came to Lisa's door, Rachel felt her head swaying. It was the same dizzy sensation that had come on a few other times during this case. She knew exactly what it was. It was a warning sign, her body's way of telling her that if she didn't slow down, she was going to end up having a full-blown episode. When she'd had one several weeks ago while chasing after a suspect, she'd managed to explain it away when Jack had asked. But she knew if it happened again, he was going to really dig in. She wondered if he might even report it to Director Anderson.

The swaying continued for a moment and even escalated. She closed her eyes against it and, though she wasn't specifically religious, found herself in something similar to prayer. *Please,* she thought. *Keep it away. Push it away. Not right now, please...*

She opened her eyes and took a deep breath. Her head was still slightly swimmy but much better than before. Still, even as she noticed

Jack's concerned gaze on her, she knew there was a ticking timebomb in her head and that it could very well knock her out at any moment.

"You good?" Jack asked.

"Yeah. Too tired, and too much adrenaline. Just some vertigo, I guess."

If he didn't buy it, he made no indication. He simply knocked on the door, but Rachel could tell by his stance that he was making sure he was ready for anything. Several seconds passed, and there was no answer. Rachel knocked the next time and again, there was no answer.

"Maybe we should call Shelby again and get Lisa's number?" Jack suggested.

Rachel considered this, but not for long. Instead, she shocked herself when she realized that she was drawing back to kick the door. Jack noticed it, too, but a moment too late.

"Rachel, what are you d—"

The first kick only caused the door to shudder in its frame. It also sent a little ache through her knee. The ache and Jack's protest nagged at her, informing her that she was going too far, that this was not standard protocol. But there was a ticking clock in her head and heart, a clock that knew she would be dead in a year. It pushed her and, ultimately, caused her not to give a shit about things like waiting on warrants or potentially overreacting and kicking a door down when a case was gnawing at her heels. She knew it went a bit beyond simply being a good agent and to something deeper, maybe something buried in her instincts and knowledge that she was indeed running on borrowed time.

Using all of this, Rachel drew back and kicked again, and then a third time. The third kick caused the edging of the frame to start cracking.

"Rachel! What the hell?"

Jack made a move to get in her way, to prevent a fourth kick. But Rachel's speed and momentum took them both by surprise. The fourth kick sent the door flying inward, taking a chunk of the frame with it. It slammed hard against something inside and bounded back, but Rachel stopped it with her hand and stepped inside.

Jack came marching in behind her and stepped in front of her. "What the hell was that? You know we don't have nearly enough evidence to cause us to forcefully enter."

"Maybe not," Rachel said, still a little surprised at herself. "But we do have four bodies, with a potential fifth on the way. Not only that, we—"

She stopped here, her eyes already scanning the apartment beyond Jack's shoulder. They were standing in the kitchen (the solid *thunk* the door had made upon flying inward had been the fridge), which gave way to the living room. From where she stood, Rachel could only see half of the couch and the coffee table, but she saw enough to cause some red flags to start waving internally.

She sidestepped Jack and made her way into the living room. The coffee table was littered with newspapers, none dated any older than the previous week. Small pieces of some were cut out, the cuts made perfectly. Partially buried under one of these cut-up pages, she saw a small pad, the sort most people used to jot down grocery lists. She knew what was on it even before she grabbed it up and had a good look.

There were a series of numbers on the pad, five in all. And four had been scratched out. Not only were they phone numbers, but Rachel even recognized two of them because she'd been staring at them constantly for the past two days: Edwin Newkirk and Joseph Staunton.

It all seemed lazy and sloppy to have it all out on the coffee table like this. But with the speed she was taking lives, Rachel supposed Lisa didn't have time to properly clean up after her morbid arts and crafts sessions.

"Jack, have a look..."

She handed him the pad, but saw that he'd also found something. The sections that had been cut from the paper had found a new home in what appeared to be a large notebook—the sort where the paper had no lines and it looked like a blend of sketchpad and portfolio. Rather than take the pad with the numbers on it from her, he held out the notebook, which he'd already opened.

She looked to the ages and saw a picture of Nicholas Harding staring out at her. In the grainy picture, he was smiling. The small headline belied that expression, though: **Local Man, 44, Jumps to Death.** Beside it, the name of the bridge he'd jumped from had been scrawled down in long, elegant strokes.

She reached out and turned the pages as Jack still held the book. The final page she came to contained an article on Dustin Adams. This one had been printed from a website. It contained a picture of the High Bridge, the bridge he'd allegedly jumped from.

"There's a fifth number here," Rachel said, shaking the pad in her hand. "I think it's safe to say that not only is Lisa the killer, but this number could very well be the fifth victim she has in mind."

131

"Yeah, I'd say that's a safe play," Jack said. He still looked a little frazzled over her kicking in the door, but he was slowly coming around. He tossed the notebook back onto its place on the couch and stood anxiously beside Rachel as she pulled out her cell phone and dialed the fifth number on the pad. She placed it on speaker mode so Jack could also hear.

The first ring sent a chill of anticipation through Rachel. Knowing that this phone call could save a life or take them directly to their killer made each ring from the other end seem like a jolt of electricity. The phone rang a second time, then a third. When the fourth ring ended abruptly and kicked over to the outgoing message, she hoped it would be the voice of the phone's owner, giving their name and asking the caller to please leave a message. Instead, they got the monotone voice of a female robot, reciting the user's phone number at them. Frustrated, Rachel killed the call. Her thoughts were rampaging through her head and she once again felt that brief flash of dizziness. She looked back to the door she'd kicked in and felt a growing tension within her. Her chest grew tight and panic started to grip her. *Great,* she thought. *A panic attack on top of everything else...*

"Rachel?"

She looked at Jack and saw that he was reaching for the pad. She handed it to him and when her arm moved, it felt like she was underwater. She was feeling far too overwhelmed. She needed to sit down. She needed to run away.

"It's okay," he said, casting a concerned look her way. "I'll get my guy at the bureau to locate the phone. We know it's a cell because of the automated outgoing message."

The idea brought Rachel out of her momentary haze. She nodded and asked, "How long do you think it'll take?"

"I'll make it clear how important it is. We can probably have a location for it in the next fifteen or twenty minutes. In the meantime, maybe we can have Branson and his men run the number and get a name for the account."

"Yeah, okay."

"Hey...Rachel. Seriously, it's okay." She could see that he was still concerned and that he was fighting the urge to ask her once again what was wrong with her.

"I know," she said. "Sorry about that, by the way," she said, pointing to the door.

"Not a problem. Seems it was your gut working overtime, and once again coming up right."

He then took out his phone and dialed up his bureau contact. Stepping a bit outside of her normal case boundaries, Rachel walked into the kitchen, found a glass in the second cupboard she checked, and ran some water out of the tap. She drank down a few mouthfuls of cold water as Jack recited the number to the man on the other line. She stared at the door she'd kicked in, still not quite sure what had come over her. Deep down, she thought she knew. She was pretty sure she wasn't taking the idea of rules and regulations very seriously anymore. She did not have a very long time left to live, so she was not going to be hampered by trivialities such as waiting for the appropriate amount of evidence to knock a door down.

She almost chuckled at the brazen understanding but managed to keep it on. Laughing in any sort of way right now, having narrowly avoided a major dizzy spell *and* a panic attack, seemed like an invitation for disaster.

Setting the glass on the edge of Lisa's sink, she took out her own phone and called Branson. When he answered, she cringed when she heard the slight bit of hope in his voice. Clearly, he was hoping for good news. And while she supposed they did have some, in a way, it wasn't the breakthrough they were all hoping for.

"We're following up with the call operator from Better Days. Her first name is Lisa and I'm ashamed to say I don't have a last name. We have a phone number I need you to see if you can find a name for. We have reason to believe it might be a very strong contender for the killer's fifth victim."

"I can't do anything with it, but I'll pass it along to someone that can."

She gave him the number and then, doing her best not to sound too pushy, she ended the call with: "Seriously. This could be huge. The sooner I can get this the better."

When she ended her call, Jack was also done with his. "Fifteen minutes," he said. "Thirty at the most."

Knowing there was no way in hell she'd be able to sit still while they waited, Rachel made her way through Lisa's apartment. It wasn't exactly ethical, but she'd already kicked a door down. What was a little snooping in the face of that? Jack said nothing about this, but his choice to stay in the living room to look at Lisa's macabre little scrapbook told her that he wasn't in agreement with it.

As Rachel looked around the bedroom, she made a small checklist in her head. They needed to call Shelby to tell her to contact them when Lisa showed up to her shift tonight—if she showed up at all. They also should probably contact Lisa's cell provider and request a copy of her phone records. There was so much that needed to be done, but the most important thing right now was locating either Lisa or the owner of that fifth number. And she had a very good feeling that one was going to lead directly to the other.

The bedroom offered up nothing, so she went into the bathroom. It was small and quaint, the sort of bathroom perfect for a woman living alone. There was no medicine cabinet, but there *were* three drawers under the sink. Rachel went through them, doing her usual search for any medications that might result in abnormal behavior. It had been a discovery that had assisted in lots of cases in the past—and it paid off here as well.

In the middle cabinet, she discovered two prescription bottles. One was Vyvanse, a standard med for treating ADHD. The other was a little more telling, though. It was Sertraline, a drug used to treat manic depressive disorders and anxiety. And seeing that prescription, the case made a whole new sense to her.

The presence of Sertraline indicated that Lisa herself had been dealing with depression. Rachel was no pharmacist, but she was pretty sure it was a medication prescribed for harsher cases of depression. She didn't think it was a stretch to assume there was a chance that Lisa may have had suicidal thoughts in the past based on this discovery. If this was this case, had she never been able to actually go through with it? Was she perhaps testing the waters or observing what it was like trough others? And if so, what better way to do that than by orchestrating such events behind the scenes?

She went into the living room to tell Jack what she'd found and to share her theory. But as she made her way back out into the hallway, she heard the familiar chirping of his cell phone. Hearing it, she raced to join him, hoping it was already his bureau contact that had been such a huge help with the phones to this point. When Jack saw her enter the room, listening to the phone and nodding, he gave her a thumbs-up.

"Thanks a ton," he told the man on the other end. "Do me a favor and keep that up for a while, okay? Let me know if it moves."

Even before he was hanging up, Jack was hurrying for the door. "I think this is it," he said. "If we act fast, we can save a life and maybe nab Lisa."

"What did you find out? Where's the phone?"

"It's moving very slowly about two miles away from where we're currently standing...on the Wards Island Bridge."

At the word *bridge*, they both took off at a steady run through the door Rachel had kicked in less than twenty minutes ago.

CHAPTER TWENTY EIGHT

With no bubble lights for their rental, Rachel had to rely on the blaring of her horn at intersections and her hazard lights. Meanwhile, Jack called on Branson to let the NYPD know where they were, where they were headed, and not to have any units try to pull them over for speeding or reckless driving. All the while, Rachel's phone was giving her directions to the bridge via GPS. It all seemed to happen quickly, not just the driving but Jack's conversation with Branson and the feeling that this case was either going to end or become a catastrophic nightmare in the next half an hour or so.

As she tore down 99th Street, slamming angrily down on the horn as she came up behind two cabs, Jack looked slightly scared of her driving but remained as professional as possible. As he spoke with Branson, an idea came to Rachel. It was insane but, at the same time, made perfect sense.

"How quick can he get a unit there?" she asked.

Jack relayed the question and parroted an answer almost immediately. "Within about five minutes. Just a little before we'd get there."

"I know it might add a few minutes, but I'm wondering if he can make it so that I have something specific waiting there for me."

"Specific like what?"

Rachel told him and his eyes grew increasingly wide. "Are you sure?"

"No. But ask anyway."

Jack shook his head in disbelief and relayed his question to Branson. When the call was over ten seconds later, Jack looked to her and nodded. "He says the equipment will be there, and he'll bring it himself. He might be several minutes behind us, though. About that equipment you wanted...I'm not sure if—"

"Me neither. But it'll work."

"It seems risky."

"I know. What else did Branson say?" she asked, trying to swerve the topic.

"He says that the Wards Island Bridge is a pedestrian bridge only. He guesses it might be about three hundred to three hundred and fifty feet tall at its highest point. There's two available units closer to the bridge than we are right now, but he said he's going to give it to us. The other units will fall in in case we need backup."

Rachel only nodded, afraid to take her eyes off of the traffic. It seemed that drivers of most of the cars they came upon did their best to get out of the way but even then, it was a major headache to get around them all.

Finally, the almost archaic shape of the Wards Island Bridge crept into view in the darkness. When she saw that the cop car that had already arrived had parked just far enough away not to attract the attention of their killer, she appreciated it. The last thing they wanted to do was tip her off.

She pulled in beside the cop car, which had parked in a small corner lot off of FDR Drive. She supposed the sight of a cop car just parked and sitting wasn't exactly an odd site, which helped to keep their cover. She rolled her window down and the cop behind the wheel of the patrol car did the same.

"You seen anything?" Rachel asked.

"Nothing. Then again, I've only been here for about five minutes. Branson told me to sit tight and wait."

"Thanks for that. And yes, Branson is on his way. What can you tell me about the bridge?"

"Pedestrian only," the cop said. "I'm pretty certain there are footpaths on both sides."

"It seems long enough so that we wouldn't be seen from this entrance," Rachel said. "Do you agree?"

The cop angled his neck back to look at the bridge and finally nodded. "Yeah, I'd say that's a safe bet. Say...you think you know who the killer is?"

"We've got a pretty good idea, yeah."

As she said this, another patrol car pulled into the lot. There were no sirens and no lights, keeping things as quiet and discreet as possible. This car pulled up alongside the passenger side of Rachel and Jack, bookending their rental between two patrol cars. Jack rolled his window down, revealing Detective Branson on the other side.

"We good to go?" Branson asked.

"Yes," Rachel said. "Did you get the stuff I asked for?"

"I did. But I have to ask—"

"Don't. Not until later. Not until this is over." She got out of the car, Jack following right along. She saw that Branson had popped the trunk of his patrol car for her. "Is my stuff in here?"

"Yeah, in a small duffel. What do you need from us?"

Rachel took the bag out, unzipped it, and looked inside. She was terrified about what she saw there, but was also filled with a reassuring feeling. Crazy or not, she thought this was really the only way to get it done…if her hunch was right.

"I need one of you to stay on this side to make sure no one leaves the bridge before we do," she answered. "How long would it take to get to the other end, on the other side of the river?"

This time of night?" Branson said. "Maybe twenty minutes. Thirty, depending on traffic."

"I need one of you to start over that way now for the same thing. If anyone tries coming off of that bridge before you see Agent Rivers or myself, you stop them."

She looked to Jack and saw that he was sending a text. As she hefted the duffel bag over her left shoulder, she heard Jack's phone ding back in response. He gave a nod and started for the bridge. "That was DC. He says the phone is still located on the bridge. We're good to go."

With that, the first cop on the scene rolled out, apparently heading to another bridge so he could get to the Randall's Island side of Wards Island Bridge. Rachel gave Branson one final look of acknowledgment before she and Jack started walking toward the bridge, which was looking over them like some dark, unguarded castle against the night.

Jack took the footpath to the right while Rachel took the one on the left. She had no idea what to expect so she kept her Glock holstered. She didn't think Lisa would be armed. She'd always just used her words as weapons, and it had been highly effective so far. As Rachel started walking along the bridge, she looked over to Jack's side and realized that he was a bit farther away than she'd anticipated. He had opted to stay just behind her and all the way against the other side of the bridge—roughly fifteen feet away.

She also started to fear that she was too late. What if sitting out in the car for those handful of minutes and waiting for Branson to arrive would be what ended up costing a fifth victim their life? What if her harebrained idea that involved the contents of the duffel bag she now carried ended up being the reason someone died?

She walked along, keeping her eyes ahead and somehow aware of the river flowing somewhere further below. The bridge slowly arched upward, making any potential jump that much deadlier. She kept her steps quick but light, nearly at a jog. He heart was tight in her chest as she looked out for any shape on the bridge ahead.

And then she saw it. About a dozen feet ahead of her, there was a single figure standing just off of the footpath. They were slightly higher than the edge of the bridge, standing out on a girder or support rail of some kind. It was hard to tell for sure in the darkness. All Rachel could tell for sure was that they were standing right on the edge, just a breath away from plunging down into the darkness, the river, and death.

CHAPTER TWENTY NINE

Rachel stopped for a moment, not sure how to proceed. If she called out, it would startle whoever was standing there and they could fall inadvertently. But if she continued to inch up closer, it could also scare them. She turned back toward Jack and held a hand out, signaling for him to stop. She didn't stop to see if he obeyed. She was too focused on the figure on the side of the bridge.

Slowly, she started walking forward again. The shape and a few details of the figure started to reveal themselves in the darkness. It appeared to be another man, quite small and wearing a windbreaker. Rachel still opted not to speak. Instead, she made a point to drag her right foot just the slightest bit as she took another step forward. Her heart slammed in her chest as she waited for the next handful of seconds to unfold.

She just hoped the person on the rail wasn't too close to the edge. If they were, the sudden sight of someone would frighten them just enough to fall.

As it turned out, the man actually took a step back in surprise when he heard the slight sound of Rachel's intentionally loud footstep. He turned to look at her but said nothing. What were you supposed to say in a situation like that, anyway? He had a dazed look on his face, like he had nearly committed to what he was about to do, but not quite yet. Being pulled from that daze, there was the slightest look of sadness in his   eyes.

"Hey there," Rachel. "Do you need some help getting down?"

"No," the man said. "I'm not getting down. I'm...I'm going to jump."

"Oh," Rachel said, doing her best to sound surprised. "Well, it's none of my business, but it seems like that would hurt."

A strained little laugh came out of the man. "Maybe you should go back so you don't have to watch."

"I would," Rachel said. "But here's the thing. I'm actually with the FBI and I have a pretty good idea that the only reason you're up there is because someone called you. Someone called you and told you this was the only way. That this was the answer. Am I right?"

"How do you...was it you? Did you call?" He looked confused, maybe a little angry. The hazy look was almost completely gone now, leaving a deeply confused man.

"No, it wasn't me. But it was a woman, wasn't it?"

"Yeah," the man said. Rachel thought he'd started laughing again, but it turned out to be weeping. He had not taken that one step back out toward the edge just yet and as far as Rachel was concerned, that was a small victory.

"I don't know what she told you, but this isn't the right way to deal with your problems. If you come down from there, I can help."

Even in the darkness, Rachel could see the man trembling from his crying. She estimated there might be about four to six inches between the edge of his foot and open air. Rachel took a subtle step forward, wondering if she may not need the items in the duffel bag after all.

"The woman who called you does not care about your best interest. She's a liar and she's been doing this very same thing to others. She doesn't know what she's talking about. Please, come down."

The man suddenly seemed almost surprised that Rachel was as close as she was. She slowly outstretched her left arm and opened her hand to him. He looked down to her and she could see the need for help, the absolute need for someone to be there for him, despite the darkness.

"I don't want to do this," he said. "My wife...she doesn't even know...and I just can't..."

"It's okay," Rachel said. She'd come to the side of the bridge now. The primary rail that served as the side of the bridge was between them, but she could still reach him. When he very slowly turned toward her, he leaned in her direction. She realized there was a very good chance that he might fall right on top of her, or on the rail. And wouldn't that be morbidly ironic if he rebounded from the rail and went falling anyway?

Rachel leaned against the edge and as the man reached for her in return, she was vaguely aware of Jack slowly coming up behind her.

"I'm her partner," he announced in a gentle tone. "I'm only here to help, too."

The presence of two people seemed to break whatever emotional bock the man was suffering from. He gave one last lean toward them, tottered for a bit, and then came sprawling forward. Rachel caught him, stumbling backwards as she did, but Jack took the brunt of it. The pain of slamming into the bridge was dull and sudden, but drowned out by the relief that she'd gotten the man down. The would-be jumper

141

scrambled to the middle of the bridge, as if making sure he was as far away from the edge as possible.

Still weeping, he looked to both of them like an embarrassed child. "I know what you must think," he said. "It's pathetic, right?"

"We weren't thinking that at all," Jack said.

"This woman was playing with your emotions," Rachel said. "She was orchestrating it for reasons we aren't sure of just yet. Given that, do you happen to know her name?"

"No. And I...I can't really talk right now. Please, I just need to get off of this fucking bridge."

"Sure thing," Jack said. "We've got two officers down below. We'll get you whatever you need."

"I'll be down in a bit," Rachel said. "I want to have a look around." What she did not say was that she found it almost impossible that Lisa would not be somewhere nearby. If she called and made this man believe he had to kill himself to make his problems go away, she'd certainly be somewhere nearby to see it happen.

"You sure?" Jack asked.

"Yeah. Just give me a minute or two."

With an uncertain nod, Jack turned away and escorted the man who had been on the brink of ending his life back down the bridge. Rachel watched them slink away, disappearing into the night.

As she watched them, the night seemed to grow silent. She could still hear the sobs of the man they'd just talked down, and the rushing water beneath them. There were the sounds of the city, sure, but they were in the background, nothing more than ambient noise.

Only, that wasn't true. There was something else. Some other sound from behind her.

Footsteps. Soft footsteps.

And they were retreating.

Rachel turned and looked down the opposite expanse of the bridge. She could not see anything in the darkness, just the open and empty bridge for about ten or twelve feet before the darkness of night took it over. She gave chase, following the sound of the retreating footsteps. Within several steps, she realized that if this was indeed the killer ahead of her, the person had made a critical mistake. Sure, there was no way the killer could know that there was currently an NYPD officer on the way to that end of the bridge, but they were trapped—about three quarters of a mile of bridge ahead of her, and a federal agent behind her.

Rachel kicked into a higher gear when she came to this realization. She also understood that the chances were very good that she was faster than the killer and, cancer diagnosis aside, in better shape. This was proven correct when she finally saw a murky shape ahead of her. It was thin shape, rushing forward in the darkness. As she closed in on the figure, Rachel could see the quickly moving legs, pumping up and down. A few more steps, and she saw the bobbing shape of a ponytail and the back of the blonde head to which it was attached.

"Lisa, stop! This is Agent Gift. I just need to talk to you!"

The figure ran for another several strides but then came to a stop. When they turned around, Rachel was not at all surprised to see Lisa, the operator from Better Days Suicide Prevention. She had a wild, almost feral look in her eyes as she stood in place, staring Rachel down as if she were an alien or monster.

"Why did you come?" Lisa asked.

"To stop you. And to see why you're doing this."

"You wouldn't understand."

"You're right," Rachel said, not giving the conversation time to breathe. She figured if she could keep things moving along quickly, she'd be able to keep Lisa from trying to run again. "You're right, I don't understand. You spend so much time trying to help these people...so why would you want to see them dead? Why would you want them to take their own lives?"

"Like I said...you wouldn't understand it." She hesitated here and the wild look melted out of her gaze. She now looked sad, almost lost. "I suppose I have a lot to answer to?"

"Yes, I won't lie about that. But right now, I just need you to come with me. Come with me and we can talk it out. We can—"

Lisa interrupted her not by speaking, but by moving swiftly to the side of the bridge. It was so unexpected that Rachel wasn't fully aware of what the woman was doing until she was crawling over the edge and out onto the outer strut.

"No! Lisa, don't do this."

Lisa got to her feet and looked back at Rachel. She was standing on the same support that the man had been standing on five minutes ago, a strut that served as the outer rail—the last flat structure on the side of the bridge before the open air took over. Rachel's only hope was that Lisa wouldn't go through with it. She suspected that she was living out some strange suicidal fantasy by talking these other people to their deaths and that she likely didn't actually have the fortitude to go through with it. But it was hard not to be afraid that she was wrong as

Lisa stood there, less than foot from letting gravity claim her body and her life.

"Please come down, Lisa. You know you don't want to do this."

"How could you know that?"

"I know that because you fooled me. You fooled me not because you lied to me when we first spoke with you but because there was concern in your voice and the way you talked about those people you've tried to help. You do care. And you're good at what you do."

Lisa seemed to consider her words for a moment, and as she did, Rachel once again became aware of the duffel bag on her shoulder. Maybe she was going to have to use what was resting inside after all.

"I'm just so tired," Lisa said, inching to the side of the strut.

"I know. You—"

"Don't do that! Don't sympathize with me. You don't even know me!"

"You're right," Rachel said. Slowly, she slid the duffel bag from her shoulder and held it in front of her. She unzipped it and took out its contents.

The bungee cord uncoiled as she lifted the harness out.

"What is that?" Lisa asked.

"It's proof that I do know how you feel. Wanting to die. Not wanting to keep on with this life. Because the truth is, you don't know me, and I don't know you. You've been keeping your depression a secret, right?"

She gave Lisa a moment to answer, though the woman remained quiet. In the silence, Rachel slipped the harness on. It went perfectly over her shoulders like a little vest. One end of the cord was already attached to the carabiner and lock on the back of the harness.

"I'm keeping a secret, too, Lisa. And it makes me want to…well, it makes me wonder what it might be like to jump. It makes me wonder what it might be like to feel that one last thing, that little bit of pain before the world slips away."

"Bullshit," Lisa said, but the tears in her voice said more than the word.

Rachel picked up the coiled bit of rope; on the phone, Branson told her that it was about eighty feet. She ran her hand through the looped cord and grabbed the other end, the clasp shining dully. "I'd really like for you to just come down off of there," Rachel said. "I really don't want to have to do this…"

"Are you nuts?" Lisa asked.

"No. A little scared, actually." She walked to the edge of the bridge, the shoulder-high metal wall now all that stood between them. She held one of three carabiners that had fallen out of the duffel bag in her left hand. She linked it through the clasp on the free end of the bungee cord and eyed the side of the bridge for somewhere the carabiner would catch.

"If I come with you, I'll go to jail, won't I?" Lisa asked. Rachel didn't think she was trying to venture into bargaining. If anything, she was hesitating just to see how far the crazy FBI agent was willing to go.

"Probably. Depends on your reasoning behind all of this—your mental state and things like that."

Along the moderate curving of the short wall, she saw a series of large bolts running along a seam. It was the sort of construction element that likely popped up at well-measured intervals all along the sides as they connected to the columns beneath. One of the bolts, the one nearest the top, ended in a rectangular opening, almost like a lock. Rachel had no idea what this was for but assumed it was to allow some sort of pulley to help loosen the bolt if the need should ever arise. It was almost too large for the carabiner, but Rachel figured it would do.

If not…well, this was going to end badly.

"Please, Lisa," she said, extending her arm and hand in the same manner she'd done for the man Lisa had talked into killing himself. "Get down from there." She stepped closer, now pressed against the side of the wall.

"No. Don't you come any closer! I'll do it!"

The scary thing was, there was the sort of dedication and grit to her voice that made Rachel sure that something had shifted in Lisa. Something was different now, and she might very well jump. Rachel saw the woman's knee bending slightly, as if she might launch herself off of the strut at any moment.

"No one will miss me," Lisa said. "I just hope the families of those people might forgive me. I hope…I hope…"

The last *hope* came out in a strangled cry. With that, Lisa gave a pleading look up to the sky. An odd expression crossed her face in that moment, a horrifying mixture of peace and fear. And it was that expression that told Rachel what was happening next.

Just as Lisa's feet bent and her body started to push itself forward toward the open air, Rachel placed her hand on the lip of the wall in front of her and heaved herself up. Seeing Lisa pivoting off of the strut, Rachel didn't have a chance to even balance herself on the wall and step out onto the strut. As Lisa went airborne, so did Rachel.

She catapulted herself off the wall and dove out over the strut Lisa had been standing on. She caught her left foot on it, sending a flare of pain through her.

It was a momentary pain, a brief flickering ache that was soon drowned out by the lack of ground and stability. That slight pain, like every other sense within Rachel's body, was overcome with a sense of absolute weightlessness as she started to fall.

CHAPTER THIRTY

It only took two seconds for Rachel to recall why she was falling. She had jumped because she'd wanted to keep Lisa from killing herself. But the sensation of falling, the wind on her face and the terrifying sense of freedom, swept her up and she momentarily forgot herself. When her mind came back to her, she frantically reached out to grab Lisa only to find that it was easier than she thought.

Their bodies had tangled slightly as they'd gone off of the bridge. Their left arms weren't quite entwined but were lapped over one another. In mid-fall, Rachel used this to her advantage and pulled Lisa's falling body against hers. In an awkward, spinning half-circle, she had to fight to get her right hand around Lisa's falling body. Her arm was nearly blocked by the bungee cord as she fought for purchase. When she finally had Lisa held tightly to her, she locked her hands over her wrists in a crude sort of chokehold around Lisa's stomach.

She got the hold locked in just as the bungee cord ran out of length. The bounce of it was much more violent than Rachel had expected. She lost her grip on Lisa but, at the same time, she locked her legs around Lisa's hips in a crude sort of MMA leg lock she'd picked up in the gym several years ago. Lisa still slid down a bit and the shock of the bungee's rebound had Rachel reeling, but Lisa was caught.

"Damn you," Lisa whimpered. She tried fighting against the lock, but it was only a half- hearted attempt. The water was no more than twenty feet beneath them now, definitely not far enough fall to do any real damage.

They bounced up and then drifted down for a second time as the bungee cord continued to sway and rebound. As it came down the second time, there was a brief sense of falling again as the cord was loosened up on the bridge. Rachel had just enough time to picture the carabiner in that oddly shaped opening within the bolt head, wondering if the carabiner had snapped or come loose, before she felt gravity take her again.

It was sudden, and both women yelled out in shock and surprise. They also flailed wildly on the way down, and Rachel caught one of Lisa's elbows to the jaw because of it. They splashed down into the water together, a tangle of legs, arms, and bungee cord.

Aside from the fresh pain in her jaw, Rachel was aware of two things: first, the current of the Harlem River was stronger than she had expected; second, her vision was littered with little white specks and the world seemed to be spinning and throbbing all around her. She had to focus an incredible amount just to move her arms and legs, trying to remind herself how to swim. When her mouth was filled with that first taste of the stagnant water of the river, it all came rushing back to her.

She stroked to the surface and did her best to locate Lisa but the world was still tottering, the disorientation made even worse by the river's current. There was the dark night sky lurking somewhere around her, and then the dark water somewhere else. She was hovering in between it all, her feet unable to find ground and her eyes unable to properly settle on anything. She did her best to make a turning motion but only made it half a circle before Lisa's weight fell on top of her. She could feel the woman's hands on top of her head, pushing her down. She went back under the water, her mouth filling with water and her vision once again streaked with those little pinpoint flashes of white light.

In the midst of those flashes, she saw Paige's face. She also saw Grandma Tate, so brave in facing down her diagnosis, so determined to enjoy the time she had left.

Ah, but she also recalled that split second of falling. She recalled leaping off of the bridge feeling weightless and absolutely *free.*

She felt Lisa pushing her down and Rachel simply stopped. She stopped fighting, she stopped trying to swim and get out from under Lisa's weight. *Maybe this is better,* she thought as her lungs started to twinge. *Maybe I just die here, away from family, without having to explain anything to anyone. Without having to go through my diagnosis with Peter and Paige, without having this cancer steal my life away, without having to go through that pain and suffering. Maybe it just ends here on my own terms...*

Again, Paige's face filled her head. She thought of Peter accidentally telling Paige about Grandma Tate. She thought of how Paige looked when she woke up first thing in the morning, of how Peter always tried cooking breakfast on Sundays and the pancake batter wasn't quite done in the center. She thought of his embrace first thing in the morning, and of Paige's laugh...

Her feet started kicking before she was aware of it. On her way to the surface, she grabbed Lisa's right arm. She twisted it and yanked up as she broke the surface. She gasped for air, her lungs aching with relief. Lisa tried to fight against her, but the arm lock made it impossible and she—

She was still so disoriented that Rachel didn't see the bright light just ahead of her. At first, her heart dropped because she was sure it was all in her head, a result of the tumor. But then she heard Lisa gasping, the fight going out of her, and then the loud roaring noise.

It was a boat. A small vessel of some kind was heading their way and the driver apparently did not see them because it was bearing down right on them. The light grew brighter, pointing off just to the right, and the engine noise was just loud enough so that she could not hear Lisa's screams as it closed in on them.

CHAPTER THIRTY ONE

The boat's light was just barely to the right of them, forging ahead and carving through the water. Now that it was nearly on top of them, Rachel could see that it wasn't a very big boat—little more than the size of a standard fishing boat—but that didn't matter; if it hit them, they were both dead. Already, she could feel the water being disrupted by its passage as the boat closed to within ten feet, then eight. The engine was like thunder, still drowning out Lisa's screams.

In a massive show of strength, using every bit of reserved energy she had, Rachel released Lisa's arm, hooked her hand along the woman's armpit, and hitched her backwards. It was a lazy sort of toss, hindered by the weight and commotion of the water. Lisa went under and the force of the toss sent Rachel backwards in what felt like a very strange aqua aerobics move, though she knew it was not nearly as graceful. She drew her legs in as quickly as she could just as the boat passed by.

She didn't feel the boat actually strike her feet, but she could feel the thrumming weight of it through the water as the wake it pushed up came crashing over her. She was tossed and pushed along by the wake, the dizzy feeling once again claiming her. However, being in the water, she knew all she had to do was kick and tilt her head in the direction she thought was up. When she broke the surface, she thought she was going to throw up. Had she ever been so tired? Had she ever felt so disoriented and at a loss of control?

Her head still reeling, she did her best to tread water while looking for Lisa. The woman was to Rachel's right, trying to swim to the shore but clearly struggling. Apparently, she was just as panicked and out of sorts as Rachel was. Rachel made a few strokes in her direction but the world continued to rock back and forth and the little white flares began to jettison across her field of vision again.

Behind her, she could barely hear the boat as the engine died down and someone onboard shouted out. Rachel gave a half-hearted wave for attention but her eyes were still on Lisa. She'd stopped trying to swim, her head going under the water. Crying out in desperation and sheer will, Rachel managed to push herself forward. The boat's wake was weaker now so it wasn't as hard to swim ahead.

"Someone help us!" she shouted as she made her way over to Lisa. Her head had completely submerged just as Rachel reached her. Reaching underwater, she felt the woman's shoulder. She hooked her finger through the fabric of the soaked shirt and pulled her up. Hugging Lisa closer to her, she treaded water and prayed she'd have enough strength. Her legs felt like jelly, her head felt like a piece of listless driftwood, and the white sparks kept blasting across her field of vision.

"Help..."

The world grew murky just as she realized that the boat that had nearly hit them was turning around, coming back for them. The driver shouted something to her but she couldn't make it out. She fought hard to keep both her and Lisa above the water but her remaining strength was draining away fast.

The world started growing dark and she felt herself slipping under the water.

She was barely aware of someone grabbing her on the back, pulling her up by the harness she was still wearing. She was then moved horizontally and placed on something flat. She still felt the rocking of the water, though, lightly back and forth. She stared up to the night sky, the shape of the Wards Island Bridge jutting out darker than the night off to her left, and after a while both shades of dark were replaced by something a bit deeper and much more calming.

***

"Rachel? Rachel, hey, come on now..."

Her eyes fluttered open. Harsh lights sliced through her eyes, so startling that she sat up with a gasp. She took in her surroundings and realized that she was in the back of an ambulance. Jack was crouched in an awkward half-bent shape over the gurney she was sitting on. She was covered in a thermal blanket, and her wet clothes were still on, though the bungee harness had been removed.

"How long?" she asked.

"Maybe fifteen minutes. You were pulled out of the river by a city maintenance boat on patrol to record river levels."

"And what about Lisa?" she asked, already slipping off of the gurney to go back outside. She kept the blanket around her shoulders.

"She's alive. She's been formally arrested, and Branson is currently taking her to the precinct. But you...well, you need to rest. I don't know what the hell you were thinking, but...well, damn. It was crazy, but it worked. She says you saved her life."

Rachel, having slid off of the gurney, hunched over to walk to the opened back doors of the ambulance. Two medics rushed to her right away. A surge of panic raced through her as she wondered if they'd be able to tell that something was wrong with her—something aside from the trauma she'd just endured and her absolute lack of strength from fighting the river and Lisa at the same time.

"I'm okay," she said. "Just tired."

"I'm sure you are," one of the medics said. She was a younger woman, maybe in her late twenties, who was currently looking at Rachel as if she were a certified badass. Rachel considered what she had just done and wondered how long it would take for word of it to spread around the bureau. She smiled tiredly as she thought of how Anderson would likely react.

"Rachel, are you really okay?" Jack asked.

"Yeah."

Jack looked to the medics and, through an appreciative smile, said: "Can we get a second?"

The medics walked away, giving them a respectful distance. One of them went to the front of the ambulance to place a call.

Jack sat on the bumper of the ambulance while Rachel reclaimed a seat on the edge of the little gurney. She held the thermal blanket tight around her shoulders not because she was cold from the river water but because it was cozy and secure.

"When Branson took her out of here," Jack said, "she begged to speak to you. She specifically asked for 'the crazy bitch that saved me' to come talk to her whenever you could." He sighed here and looked in the direction of the river. "As your partner and friend, I want to suggest that might be a very bad idea."

"But we need to an actual confession out of her and if she—"

"Oh, we got one. She admitted to all of it right in front of me, Branson, and two other cops. She said she only ever started volunteering because she liked to hear people's plans about suicide. She'd wanted to kill herself for years but never had the courage. She arranged these events to live vicariously through them. And it was just like you figured. Harding and Staunton actually went through with it. But Newkirk and Adams needed some extra help. She even admitted to pushing Adams off of the High Bridge and knowing his head struck the side when he fell."

"And she just admitted to all of it?"

He nodded, giving her a concerned look. "I'm not sure what it is you're going through, but I'm starting to think it goes beyond what you

152

told me about your grandmother. And after this case we just went through, I don't think it's a good idea to have an audience with a woman who is clearly quite gifted in using her words—whether it's to talk someone down from suicidal thoughts or to kick them into gear. You caught her and she's been arrested. There's no use in talking to her."

There were so many questions she wanted Lisa to answer but she knew Jack was right. The fact that Lisa had been adamant about speaking with her after being pulled from the river even suggested that she had some sort of devious plan in mind. And quite frankly, Rachel didn't have the capacity for it.

"She'll need to be placed on suicide watch," she commented.

"And you can recommend that when we wrap it all up tomorrow. But please just stay away from her. I think we're done with this case outside of reports and paperwork."

When Rachel nodded in agreement, she found it hard to keep her head up. "I need to sleep," she said. It sounded like a childish request but she felt it from the very core of her soul. She was so tired, so confused and disoriented. And really, as she recalled those flickering white lights and the swaying of her head while in the river, she was also scared.

"Will you let the medics look you over first?" Jack asked.

"Just a basic look-over. I'm not going to the hospital."

"That's what I figured you'd say. I'll get them for you." He got up from the bumper and started walking away but stopped as he came to the side of the ambulance. He turned back to her and, with more emotion that she'd ever seen from him, gave one last thought. "When they pulled you out of the water and onto that boat, I thought you were dead. Until I ran down to the bank and saw you breathing, there were three or four minutes where I was sure you were dead. I don't mind saying that it terrified me and it hurt more than I was ready to handle. I'm only telling you this so I can once again let you know that I'm here for you. If there's anything at all you need to tell me or anything you're struggling with...Rachel, I'm here for you."

The truth of the last three weeks was on her tongue, ready to be spilled. The truth about her diagnosis, the truth about her passing out and the dizzy spells. But in the end, she swallowed it down. It would have to be Peter and Paige first. And then maybe Jack.

"I know, Jack. And I appreciate it. But I'm good for now."

She saw the slight stab of hurt cross his face before he rounded the corner to fetch the medics. And while he was gone, Rachel's eyes crept back up to the bridge and recalled what it had been like to fall—so weightless, inviting, and free.

CHAPTER THIRTY TWO

Rachel tacked the old bedsheet into the post of the back porch, making sure it was stretched tight. Behind her, Peter was running an extension cord from the back door and out into the yard. They'd set up the old projector at Paige's request, as she wanted a movie night in the back yard. They'd done this before, casting a movie via the projector onto the white bed sheet, and it was one of Paige's favorite things to do as a family. Even when they told her she could invite a friend, she always declined because she wanted it to just be the three of them.

"Mom!" Paige voice said through the partially opened back door. "Is it okay if we use the Mega-Butter popcorn?"

"Yes, sweetie, that's fine!"

With the sheet hung, she looked to the sky. It would be at least another forty-five minutes before it was dark enough to see anything from the projector. Frowning, she hurried up the porch steps and back inside. She caught Paige just as she was about to put the popcorn into the microwave.

"Hold off just a bit, would you? I don't think it's quite dark enough yet."

"I didn't think so either. I just really wanted some popcorn."

Rachel smiled and put the bag of kernels in herself. "Fine. Just don't complain when we're out of snacks halfway through the movie."

"Well, what about the cookies? We can use those, too."

"Cookies? My gosh, are you trying to get a tummy ache?"

She'd been home for three days and had yet to tell Peter about the harder aspects of the case. Her moment in the river had been frightening and typically, whenever she felt her life had been in danger, she told Peter just so he was kept up to date. She looked out the window and saw him hooking the projector into his laptop on the picnic table. As she watched him work so diligently to put his daughter's perfect night together, something both beautiful and frightening settled over Rachel's heart. This was her family, everything she loved. She cared for these people and they cared for her. To keep such a massive secret from them was a betrayal of the special bond they shared. It would hurt, yes. But they'd hurt together. They'd figure it out together.

It's time.

"Hey, Paige, do you think you could go clean your room for a minute or two?"

"What? But the movie!"

"We'll still watch it, you silly goose. This way you won't have to do it Saturday. And we have to wait until it gets dark anyway."

Paige considered this for a second and nodded. "Cleaning my room on a Friday evening is weird. You and Daddy just need to have a grown-up talk, don't you?"

"Yes, we do."

"Is it about Grandma Tate? Because I can hear that. Daddy told me, you know."

"I know. And that's something we're all going to talk about soon— as a family, together. But for right now, I do need to have a talk with Daddy."

"Okay. Can I come down to get the popcorn when it's done?"

"Yes. But don't spill it all over your room."

Paige grinned and took off in the direction of the stairs. Rachel listened to her little footfalls thundering along on each step. She then heard one of the Twenty-One Pilots songs Paige had been obsessed with lately as she started cleaning her room.

When Rachel headed back outside, her heart felt like it weighed about ten tons, just floating around in a chaotic sea of nerves. She walked slowly down the stairs and to the picnic table. She sat down as Peter started to scroll through the Family selections on Disney Plus.

"Did Her Highness tell you which movie we'll be watching?" Peter asked.

"No, not yet. She's too focused on popcorn."

"Ah, the priorities of a child."

Peter came around to the bench seat on her side of the picnic table and put his arm around her. "You okay?" he asked. "I hope it's okay to say so, but you've been a little off since you got back home. I figured it had something to do with that Alex Lynch creep calling me."

In the last few days, with the case in New York ending the way it had and her scary moment in the river, Alex's call had nearly escaped her mind. But now that his name had come out of Peter's mouth here in their back yard, it brought it all roaring back with violent force. She managed to shove it to the side, though, not wanting to get distracted from what she really needed to tell him.

In that same way, she also decided not to tell him about her life-threatening moment in the Harlem River. Not yet, anyway. She knew deep down that if she led with that, she'd leave it there. His reaction to such a harrowing moment would surely cause her to put the news of her diagnosis on the back burner. Really, she'd be like Lisa in that she'd be so close to the edge and taking that jump, only to back away and distract herself with something else.

"No, it wasn't Alex. But that *is* alarming and I still need to get to the bottom of how he got your number and was able to make the call. But, Peter…there is something I need to talk to you about."

She turned to him and did everything she could to keep her nerves and tears away. She wanted to reach out and take his hand, but even with the weight of what she had to tell him, it seemed like a cheesy gesture.

He was already concerned. His eyes were deep and searching. It seemed as if he already knew something bad was on the way. "Is it about my slipping up about the Grandma Tate thing? I figured we'd need to sort that out sometime soon."

"No, it's not that either." She took a deep breath and, in the end, did end up taking his hand.

"There was a morning just over three weeks ago when I was out at the training fields. I was running one of the courses, just a sort of routine exercise that I've done several times before. I had it in my head that I was going to beat my own time and maybe even the course's best time. And I think I might have done it. I really do. But just before I got—"

She was interrupted by a scream that instantly brought her to her feet.

Paige. Paige was screaming, and it was not a playful and overexaggerated scream she often used when playing. This was the sound of her daughter terrorized by something, and it had Rachel sprinting across the yard as quickly as her feet would carry her. When she blasted through the back door, she was only vaguely aware of Peter trying to keep up with her.

Paige was still shrieking when Rachel sped through the kitchen and into the hall. "Paige! What is it, baby?" she yelled as she took the stairs two at a time.

"Mommy!" The shrieking was laced with tears now, the screams sharp and punctuated. And then there were little footfalls as she came running out of her room.

Rachel met her in the hallway. There were tears in her eyes and she held her hands out in front of her as if she were afraid to touch anything.

"What is it?" Rachel asked. "Are you hurt? Are you okay?"

Paige nodded, but kept looking at her hands as little tears rolled down her cheeks. "Something in my room," she said through a series of whines. "I didn't mean to touch it, but I was cleaning up and wanted to see and…"

Peter came up behind them and huddled around as well. "What is it?"

"Daddy…" Paige said, hugging him.

Rachel started for her daughter's bedroom with the same kind of gait in which she'd approach a mysterious room during a case. The door was open and as she stepped inside, the mother instincts that had seen far too many freak-outs over small things was fully expecting there to be a spider on the floor or maybe even a bee buzzing around.

But she saw what had her daughter in tears right away. It was over by the window, just a few feet away from Paige's little pink toy chest. Her heart went cold as she walked over to it, and colder still when she knelt down by it.

There was a dead squirrel on Paige's floor. Its neck was broken, the head turned nearly all the way around. It had also been gutted, cut from neck to crotch with its innards hanging out. It was recent violence, the blood fresh and the guts still wet and glistening.

A small scrap of paper had been crammed in where the entrails should have been. Without even thinking about it, Rachel plucked the paper out and unfolded it. It appeared to be a sticky note, all crumpled up to fit inside the small space

"Rachel?" Peter called out from the hallway. "What is it?"

She didn't answer. She straightened out the paper and found a note inside. It was written in very tiny script and the paper had become softened by the blood and fluids. She started to tremble, already quite certain what she was going to find but not sure how it was possible. The note read:

Tell your secret, or I will. Take a lesson from Mr. Squirrel and spill your guts.
Your Friend,
Alex Lynch

She dropped the note to the floor and looked at the squirrel. There were far too many questions, chief among them being how the hell Alex Lynch had gotten into her daughter's room. But those questions would have to wait. Even now, she heard Peter's footsteps coming toward the room.

She felt a hot, piercing hatred of Alex Lynch as Peter called her name again while approaching the doorway. She'd been on the cusp of telling him about her diagnosis but now Alex Lynch had ruined that. And by somehow delivering this sick gift and note, he'd ruined so much more. He'd ruined the very core and essence of her family.

Peter appeared in the doorway with Paige hugging his leg. "What is it?" Peter asked. Then, seeing the look of fear on her face, he added: "Jesus, Rachel, what's going on?"

She felt sick as she took in a deep breath but somehow, while standing in front of the squirrel and blocking it from their sight, Rachel knew it was time to do exactly as the note had suggested.

It was time to tell him everything.

NOW AVAILABLE!

HER LAST HOPE
(A Rachel Gift FBI Suspense Thriller —Book 3)

A serial killer is targeting vulnerable organ donors with seemingly no rhyme or reason, and Rachel is locked in a furious race against time to find the connection between the murders and stop him before he strikes again.

FBI Special Agent Rachel Gift is among the FBI's most brilliant agents at hunting down serial killers. She plans on doing this forever—until she discovers she has months left to live. Determined to go down fighting, and to keep her diagnosis a secret, Rachel faces her own mortality while trying to save other's lives. But how long can she go until she collapses under the weight of it all?

"A MASTERPIECE OF THRILLER AND MYSTERY. Blake Pierce did a magnificent job developing characters with a psychological side so well described that we feel inside their minds, follow their fears and cheer for their success. Full of twists, this book will keep you awake until the turn of the last page."
--Books and Movie Reviews, Roberto Mattos (re Once Gone)

HER LAST HOPE (A Rachel Gift FBI Suspense Thriller) is book #3 in a long-anticipated new series by #1 bestseller and USA Today bestselling author Blake Pierce, whose bestseller Once Gone (a free download) has received over 1,000 five star reviews.

FBI Agent Rachel Gift, 33, unparalleled for her ability to enter the minds of serial killers, is a rising star in the Behavioral Crimes Unit—until a routine doctor visit reveals she has but a few months left to live.

Not wishing to burden others with her pain, Rachel decides, agonizing as it is, not to tell anyone—not even her boss, her partner, her husband, or her seven-year-old daughter. She wants to go down fighting, and to take as many serial killers with her as she can.

When a series of different organ donors are murdered, Rachel is determined to track down the killer. But Rachel herself is faltering, beginning to succumb to her illness. Can she keep it together long enough to catch this killer before her own death? And can she keep her own demons—and her own traumatic past—at bay?

A riveting and chilling crime thriller featuring a brilliant and flailing FBI agent, the RACHEL GIFT series is an unputdownable mystery, packed with suspense, twists and shocking secrets, propelled by a page-turning pace that will keep you bleary-eyed late into the night.

Books #4-#6 are also available!

Blake Pierce

Blake Pierce is the USA Today bestselling author of the RILEY PAGE mystery series, which includes seventeen books. Blake Pierce is also the author of the MACKENZIE WHITE mystery series, comprising fourteen books; of the AVERY BLACK mystery series, comprising six books; of the KERI LOCKE mystery series, comprising five books; of the MAKING OF RILEY PAIGE mystery series, comprising six books; of the KATE WISE mystery series, comprising seven books; of the CHLOE FINE psychological suspense mystery, comprising six books; of the JESSE HUNT psychological suspense thriller series, comprising nineteen books; of the AU PAIR psychological suspense thriller series, comprising three books; of the ZOE PRIME mystery series, comprising six books; of the ADELE SHARP mystery series, comprising thirteen books, of the EUROPEAN VOYAGE cozy mystery series, comprising four books; of the new LAURA FROST FBI suspense thriller, comprising six books (and counting); of the new ELLA DARK FBI suspense thriller, comprising nine books (and counting); of the A YEAR IN EUROPE cozy mystery series, comprising nine books, of the AVA GOLD mystery series, comprising six books (and counting); and of the RACHEL GIFT mystery series, comprising six books (and counting).

An avid reader and lifelong fan of the mystery and thriller genres, Blake loves to hear from you, so please feel free to visit www.blakepierceauthor.com to learn more and stay in touch.

BOOKS BY BLAKE PIERCE

RACHEL GIFT MYSTERY SERIES
HER LAST WISH (Book #1)
HER LAST CHANCE (Book #2)
HER LAST HOPE (Book #3)
HER LAST FEAR (Book #4)
HER LAST CHOICE (Book #5)
HER LAST BREATH (Book #6)

AVA GOLD MYSTERY SERIES
CITY OF PREY (Book #1)
CITY OF FEAR (Book #2)
CITY OF BONES (Book #3)
CITY OF GHOSTS (Book #4)
CITY OF DEATH (Book #5)
CITY OF VICE (Book #6)

A YEAR IN EUROPE
A MURDER IN PARIS (Book #1)
DEATH IN FLORENCE (Book #2)
VENGEANCE IN VIENNA (Book #3)
A FATALITY IN SPAIN (Book #4)

ELLA DARK FBI SUSPENSE THRILLER
GIRL, ALONE (Book #1)
GIRL, TAKEN (Book #2)
GIRL, HUNTED (Book #3)
GIRL, SILENCED (Book #4)
GIRL, VANISHED (Book 5)
GIRL ERASED (Book #6)
GIRL, FORSAKEN (Book #7)
GIRL, TRAPPED (Book #8)
GIRL, EXPENDABLE (Book #9)

LAURA FROST FBI SUSPENSE THRILLER
ALREADY GONE (Book #1)
ALREADY SEEN (Book #2)

ALREADY TRAPPED (Book #3)
ALREADY MISSING (Book #4)
ALREADY DEAD (Book #5)
ALREADY TAKEN (Book #6)

EUROPEAN VOYAGE COZY MYSTERY SERIES
MURDER (AND BAKLAVA) (Book #1)
DEATH (AND APPLE STRUDEL) (Book #2)
CRIME (AND LAGER) (Book #3)
MISFORTUNE (AND GOUDA) (Book #4)
CALAMITY (AND A DANISH) (Book #5)
MAYHEM (AND HERRING) (Book #6)

ADELE SHARP MYSTERY SERIES
LEFT TO DIE (Book #1)
LEFT TO RUN (Book #2)
LEFT TO HIDE (Book #3)
LEFT TO KILL (Book #4)
LEFT TO MURDER (Book #5)
LEFT TO ENVY (Book #6)
LEFT TO LAPSE (Book #7)
LEFT TO VANISH (Book #8)
LEFT TO HUNT (Book #9)
LEFT TO FEAR (Book #10)
LEFT TO PREY (Book #11)
LEFT TO LURE (Book #12)
LEFT TO CRAVE (Book #13)

THE AU PAIR SERIES
ALMOST GONE (Book#1)
ALMOST LOST (Book #2)
ALMOST DEAD (Book #3)

ZOE PRIME MYSTERY SERIES
FACE OF DEATH (Book#1)
FACE OF MURDER (Book #2)
FACE OF FEAR (Book #3)
FACE OF MADNESS (Book #4)
FACE OF FURY (Book #5)
FACE OF DARKNESS (Book #6)

WATCHING (Book #1)
WAITING (Book #2)
LURING (Book #3)
TAKING (Book #4)
STALKING (Book #5)
KILLING (Book #6)

RILEY PAIGE MYSTERY SERIES
ONCE GONE (Book #1)
ONCE TAKEN (Book #2)
ONCE CRAVED (Book #3)
ONCE LURED (Book #4)
ONCE HUNTED (Book #5)
ONCE PINED (Book #6)
ONCE FORSAKEN (Book #7)
ONCE COLD (Book #8)
ONCE STALKED (Book #9)
ONCE LOST (Book #10)
ONCE BURIED (Book #11)
ONCE BOUND (Book #12)
ONCE TRAPPED (Book #13)
ONCE DORMANT (Book #14)
ONCE SHUNNED (Book #15)
ONCE MISSED (Book #16)
ONCE CHOSEN (Book #17)

MACKENZIE WHITE MYSTERY SERIES
BEFORE HE KILLS (Book #1)
BEFORE HE SEES (Book #2)
BEFORE HE COVETS (Book #3)
BEFORE HE TAKES (Book #4)
BEFORE HE NEEDS (Book #5)
BEFORE HE FEELS (Book #6)
BEFORE HE SINS (Book #7)
BEFORE HE HUNTS (Book #8)
BEFORE HE PREYS (Book #9)
BEFORE HE LONGS (Book #10)
BEFORE HE LAPSES (Book #11)
BEFORE HE ENVIES (Book #12)
BEFORE HE STALKS (Book #13)

BEFORE HE HARMS (Book #14)

AVERY BLACK MYSTERY SERIES
CAUSE TO KILL (Book #1)
CAUSE TO RUN (Book #2)
CAUSE TO HIDE (Book #3)
CAUSE TO FEAR (Book #4)
CAUSE TO SAVE (Book #5)
CAUSE TO DREAD (Book #6)

KERI LOCKE MYSTERY SERIES
A TRACE OF DEATH (Book #1)
A TRACE OF MURDER (Book #2)
A TRACE OF VICE (Book #3)
A TRACE OF CRIME (Book #4)
A TRACE OF HOPE (Book #5)

Made in the USA
Columbia, SC
16 July 2022